A special note of interest to the reader

Harlequin Books were first published in 1949. The original book was entitled "The Manatee" and was identified as Book No. 1 — since then over seventeen hundred titles have been published, each numbered in sequence.

As readers are introduced to Harlequin Romances, very often they wish to obtain older titles. In the main, these books are sought by number, rather than necessarily by title or author.

To supply this demand, Harlequin prints an assortment of "old" titles every year, and these are made available to all bookselling stores via special Harlequin Jamboree displays.

As these books are exact reprints of the original Harlequin Romances, you may indeed find a few typographical errors, etc., because we apparently were not as careful in our younger days as we are now. None the less, we hope you enjoy this "old" reprint, and we apologize for any errors you may find.

WELCOME
TO THE WONDERFUL WORLD
of Harlequin Romances!

Interesting, informative and entertaining, each Harlequin Romance portrays an appealing love story. Harlequin Romances take you to faraway places — places with real people facing real love situations — and you become part of their story.

As publishers of Harlequin Romances, we're extremely proud of our books (we've been publishing them since 1954). We're proud also that Harlequin Romances are North America's most-read paperback romances.

Eight new titles are released every month and are sold at nearly all book-selling stores across Canada and the United States.

A free catalogue listing all available Harlequin Romances can be yours by writing to the

HARLEQUIN READER SERVICE,
M.P.O. Box 707, Niagara Falls, N.Y. 14302.
Canadian address: Stratford, Ontario, Canada.

or use order coupon at back of book.

We sincerely hope you enjoy reading this Harlequin Romance.

Yours truly,
THE PUBLISHERS
Harlequin Romances

SHEILA OF CHILDREN'S WARD

by

MARGARET BAUMANN

HARLEQUIN BOOKS   TORONTO WINNIPEG

Original hard cover edition published in 1964
by Mills & Boon Limited.

© Margaret Baumann 1964

Harlequin edition published June 1964

Reprinted 1974

All the characters in this book have no existence outside the imagination of the Author, and have no relation whatsoever to anyone bearing the same name or names. They are not even distantly inspired by any individual known or unknown to the Author, and all the incidents are pure invention.

The Harlequin trade mark, consisting of the word HARLEQUIN and the portrayal of a Harlequin, is registered in the United States Patent Office and in the Canada Trade Marks Office.

Printed in Canada

CHAPTER I

'Then there's Gino,' said Sheila.

Dr Sawley stirred his coffee vigorously and looked thoughtful.

'You're certainly up against something there.'

'He's so little and so lost.' Sheila's voice went unsteady. 'I could help him, but he won't let me.'

His full name was Gino Cort. He was eight years old. He'd been here in the Children's Ward months and months with acute rheumatism and complications, and Sheila had been told no one ever came to see him. He seemed to her the loneliest little boy in the world, and what twisted her heart was the smouldering distrust in the pair of enormous brown eyes that stared at her out of his small, pale face.

'This is my first morning, and he hates me already!'

'Now look, you mustn't get a thing about Gino,' said Dr Sawley. 'He's the same with all of us. Life has pushed him around and he just ain't going to trust nobody no more. That's the way it is. Even that scatty little Irish nurse can't make him smile. And you can't blame the foster-mother for not popping in to see him. She used to, at first. But all Gino had for her was a string of swear-words that made Sister Bain's hair stand on end, believe you me.'

Sheila frowned.

'He's learnt those swear-words from someone!' she accused.

'Not from me he hasn't,' said Dr Sawley virtuously.

His eyes were twinkling. He was a fair-haired lad with a stethoscope slung round his neck and the pocket of his white coat bristling with fountain pen, patella hammer, a bunch of charts—the lot. Sheila guessed this junior house job was his first post since graduating from medical school.

He was conscientious and friendly and he'd taken time off, midway through a hectically busy morning, to join her for coffee. He gave her his nice smile now and said: 'You'll really get somewhere with the other kids, though. Boredom is the great enemy. And here you are with no end of fun and games up your sleeve.'

'So far,' Sheila had to confess ruefully, 'I just feel in the way.'

'Hey, none of that! You'll be doing a fine job. Me, I'm *for* you.'

Sheila knew that already and was grateful. No one else had made the slightest effort to set her at ease. It was hard to believe this was the red-letter day she had looked forward to so eagerly.

Three months ago she had thrown up her post teaching music and handwork at a junior school in the south. Her father had suffered a heart attack, and though she and her mother had nursed him safely through the critical early days, he was still rather frail and precarious. The damage was done; from now on he must always take care, and that irked him. He hadn't demanded any sacrifice of Sheila, but in a thousand little ways she had come to understand how much both her parents had missed her during the three years she'd been away; what a happiness it would be to them if she found a post nearer home.

And why not? Junior schools were crying out for staff. She could have her pick of jobs. But somehow, after the upheaval of her father's illness, she felt restless and unsettled. No ordinary job would do. She was in this frame of mind when she chanced on an advertisement in the local paper, the *Marbury Gazette*, and read it aloud at the tea-table. The General Hospital needed a teacher for the Children's Ward. 'Practical young woman with strong sense of humour.'

'That's me,' said Sheila.

Her mother smiled.

'I know your work is practical, Sheila dear, but at

heart you're such a dreamer.' She began picking holes in the job. 'You'd be on your own. No chance of promotion. And you'd see such harrowing things. Many of the children must be too ill for lessons.'

'Set lessons—yes. But I could keep them busy and happy. Warm the atmosphere for them, so to speak.'

'Now if it were a modern building in the country . . . But that grim red brick place in a dingy part of the town! It looks more like a prison than a hospital.'

James Thorne put in: 'Perhaps that's how it seems to the kids. Since I've been ill and had time hang so heavy on my hands I can imagine what a stay in hospital means to a lively child. Mind you, the job isn't every girl's cup of tea.'

'Strong sense of humour,' Sheila murmured. 'That's the sugar to sweeten the tea, I suppose!' She handed her cup across the table and said firmly: 'Three lumps, please. I'm going to have a go at it.'

No harm in applying, and she might not land it, anyway.

It was rather a shock to find herself the only applicant. And there was another shock at her interview with the Hospital Committee, when a couple of old diehards, Mr Porson and Mr Mercks, did their best to have the appointment 'referred back', even at that late stage. It was all very well, they said bluntly, for a special children's hospital or convalescent home to employ a full-time teacher; but in a general hospital it was 'one of these costly new notions' that needed thinking about before they rushed into it.

'Rubbish!' Dr Alexander Gannet, the children's specialist whose fame extended far beyond Marbury, glared round the committee table. He was a dapper little man with a large, pale, clever face and thinning dark hair. 'Haven't we children who are bored and homesick during a short stay that scarcely gives them chance to settle down with us? And what about our long-stay children—our burns, our orthopaedic cases, our anaemias? Matron is short of staff. She can't spare nurses to entertain the children all day long.'

Mr Porson seemed about to interrupt and was nipped in the bud by Dr Gannet's uplifted hand.

'I know what you're going to say, sir. There's such a thing as voluntary service. This retired headmistress, Miss Furlong, has come in twice a week or so to read aloud to the children, and we're enormously grateful. From time to time friends of the hospital put on some entertainment, notably at Christmas, and Sister Bain has her little fund for birthday treats and such special occasions. Also, of course, the mothers are encouraged to look in at teatime, but that doesn't rule out the need for a trained teacher. No, not by any means.'

The Children's Ward, he said, staring hard at Mr Porson and Mr Mercks, was the Cinderella of Marbury General.

When he shook hands with Sheila after the interview he made her feel her job was vital. He had this tremendous enthusiasm and between them they would achieve splendid things for the children. But she caught a baleful glance from Mr Porson and knew that if ever he could do her a bad turn, she was for it.

But she hadn't been thinking of Mr Porson this fresh spring morning when she passed with a light, eager step under the gloomy red arches of the hospital entrance. She had to weave across a yard where cars were parked and where a bed of wallflowers, bowed and battered by the hard winter, now struggled against the city grime and smog. From the yard she entered a sort of tunnel and followed a maze of corridors to the Children's Ward. There were swing doors and a short passage off which opened the kitchen and linen-room and Sister's office. Then more swing doors opening on the big ward which was done in butter yellow with a topping of cream and had a long sun balcony down one side.

All this was much as she had pictured. It was the noise that took her by surprise. 'Housewives' Choice' was on very loud, and near at hand there was a clatter of washing up. Babies were crying, children running about in red flannel dressing gowns with MGH embroidered in white on the pocket or calling to one another shrilly from bed to bed.

Panic surged up. Only the thought of Dr Gannet's faith in her kept her from bolting. The minute she saw him everything would be all right. *Of course*.

She stood hesitating in the door of Sister Bain's office, a slim girl of twenty-three with wide hazel eyes in which little sparks of laughter danced like the bubbles in champagne. Her face was framed by a lot of soft brown hair which the wind had blown into a tangle as she crossed the yard. She was laden like a donkey with a portable easel to serve as blackboard, a large roll of drawing paper, an old attaché case bursting with treasures and an awkward handful of twigs—cherry and horse-chestnut and elm—on which the buds of spring were sticky and bursting. She also carried, if not a lamp, at least a small and humble torch, though this of course was invisible to Sister Bain whom she'd caught at a busy and harassing moment.

She smiled hopefully. 'Doctor Gannet?'

'Doctor Gannet?' Sister Bain repeated it. She sounded surprised and a little shocked. 'Oh, no. I'm afraid he isn't here.'

'He isn't here!' Sheila echoed in a flat, dismayed voice. She had taken it for granted the Chief would make a point of welcoming her and explaining the set-up, for this job had such special problems. 'Never mind, I expect he'll be in later.'

Sister Bain gave her a funny look.

'He won't be in all week. He's in Switzerland at a medical congress.'

Sheila made a little choked sound. All her hopes ran out with a gurgle like the bath water.

'Dim of me, wasn't it, to imagine he'd be on the spot at nine on a Monday morning like a sort of headmaster!

If you had the consultants under foot at this hour you'd never get straight.'

Sister Bain, who was short and compact, her fresh complexion set off by the royal blue dress and muslin cap, looked offended.

'We're as straight as one ever is with children. A hospital day starts early, Miss Thorne. My nurses jump to it at seven-thirty when we take over the ward from the night staff.'

It was actually a relief when the telephone rang and she was left standing while Sister sat down at the desk and made notes on a pad.

I'm not wanted here, Sheila thought miserably. It couldn't have been made plainer. Yes, without Dr Gannet she was lost.

Just when her spirits were at the lowest ebb the ward doors suddenly flapped open and a scraggy little boy was catapulted out. He hurled himself at Sheila and grasped her round the knees. Laden as she was, he nearly threw her off balance. A nurse in mauve stripes came hurrying out after him, scolding in a rich Irish brogue. And at the same moment Sister Bain reappeared, a list in her hand and her eyebrows way up in her hair.

'Really, Staff, this is disgraceful. We'll have them running home next!'

The small boy announced in piercing tones: 'I won't have a prick. I won't! I won't!'

'Isn't he the spalpeen now?' said the staff nurse. 'I'd only be turning me back half a jiffy, Sister, that's holy truth.'

'Half a jiffy too long,' said Sister severely. But as she bent to the child, a change came into her face. Sheila saw warmth and compassion there. 'Come now, what's a little prick?' Then, to the nurse, in her no-nonsense tone: 'When Jackie has had his insulin, Staff, I want you to pre-med the fractured tibia. Theatre has just rung down. I'm about to check the list.'

'I will so, Sister.'

'And if you can find a minute, show Miss Thorne round and let her meet the children.'

The nurse grabbed Jackie and the doors flapped behind them. Sheila's throat had gone tight. She whispered: 'Poor little chap!'

Sister said briskly: 'The injection doesn't worry him the least bit. He couldn't squeeze out a tear, or didn't you notice? This was just a little diversion because he wants to be made a fuss of. If you can keep the children from tripping up my nurses all day long, Miss Thorne, that'll be something.'

Sheila plucked up courage.

'I'm hoping to do more than that, Sister. I've read Doctor Gannet's books on child health and I think he has the most wonderful ideas.'

Sister gave her another of those funny looks and said dryly:

'He has indeed. And now you must excuse me. This theatre list is urgent. Monday is murder, you know. Well, you'll want somewhere to keep your bits and bats.' Perhaps she didn't mean that to sound so disparaging. Her gaze came to rest on the bunch of twigs. 'And a vase for these. Or are they dead?'

Not as dead as my hopes, thought Sheila, flushing painfully.

'A jug, a jam-jar. Anything will do.'

Sister Bain glanced across the passage and called: 'Nurse Velta!'

A Jamaican girl wearing the handkerchief cap of a student nurse was emptying a laundry hamper. She stood to attention with a pile of sheets in her arms.

'Sister ma'am?'

'Empty the low cupboard for Miss Thorne's stuff.'

'Yes, Sister ma'am.' She dropped the whole lot of sheets back in the hamper.

'Finish your task first, Nurse, for goodness' sake. And when you stack that linen on the shelves, don't forget it's the folded edge outwards.'

'Yes, Sister ma'am,' came in muffled tones from deep in the hamper.

Turning back to her office, Sister Bain spared Sheila one more precious minute.

'You'll soon know your way around.' She paused. 'I'll give you a hint. It pays to keep on the right side of the Registrar. He has a lot of responsibility while the Chief is away.' Then, suddenly human: 'Talk about throwing his weight around!'

The phone rang again. She was speaking primly into the instrument.

'Yes, Doctor. Certainly, Doctor.' Then, in sudden agitation: 'You're admitting three cases from the clinic? Two of them broncho-pneumonias? Yes, I got that. But where am I to find beds for them? We're chock-a-block . . . Yes, Doctor. Of course, Doctor.'

She was up to the eyes in it. They all were. No one had time for the ward teacher.

Her heart hot and miserable, Sheila went to take possession of the only place Sister Bain had found for her, the low cupboard.

❈　❈　❈

Being shown round by Nurse Connell was like making a sightseeing tour on roller skates. Jackie in his red dressing gown followed them round, making puffing and snorting noises.

'I'm on lines,' he said importantly, the ordeal of the prick already forgotten.

'Railway lines?' Sheila said.

'Red and black lines,' said Jackie.

'It's his diet,' Nurse Connell explained. 'Och, the boy still loses weight in spite of everything. He has us powerful worried.'

But who'd have guessed it, thought Sheila. The only thing that seemed to weigh on their minds was Dr Gannet's Registrar admitting three cases from his outpatient clinic when the ward was 'chock-a-block' already.

They skated past the babies' wing and the two small glass rooms where critically ill cases were nursed close under Sister's eye with strict precautions against cross-infection.

'No through traffic,' said Nurse Connell. 'And if ye'd so much as peep at the babies without a sterile gown and mask, Red would be having your blood, he would so.'

'The Registrar?'

'That's right. He's the Boss Man round this place.' Nurse Connell rolled up her eyes. 'He'd have us with our noses to the autoclave while the Chief's away. And 'tis the hard word he'd be giving us, however we try to please the man!'

Just let him try bossing me, thought Sheila with sudden fire. The nurses might scurry round in fear of a ticking off from this bully, and even Sister Bain might put on a meek tone to him over the telephone. She herself was answerable only to Dr Gannet and the Management Committee. She intended making that absolutely clear from the start. But as for planning out a scheme of work and play for the ward, she was full of misgivings. There were too many children to teach individually, and she didn't see how to get them organized in groups. The beds were not arranged by ages. The orthopaedic cases, both boys and girls, were at one side of the ward and medical cases at the other, but there were gaps where beds had been moved out on the balcony for the day. And some young children who were able to be out of bed were playing with bricks and puzzles at a low table or squabbling for a go on the battered old rocking horse.

'We whisk every blessed one into bed before old Red does his round,' said Nurse Connell. 'Sister has a jar of barley sugar sweeties and it comes in powerful handy at a time like that. Sawley's a good sport—he's the houseman—and has fun with the kids. But himself likes to find the ward tiddly and shipshape when he comes in.'

Sheila was sure he did. The man sounded quite insufferable.

Of course there were cases that never cluttered up the place at all. Norina, for instance. She was a teenager, dreadfully thin and with a waxy pallor from some obscure form of anaemia. She had a picture paper propped in front of her and a gallery of pop singers above the bed. A rough piece of cardboard on which she had crudely drawn out *I love Elvis* had the place of honour.

There was Stephen, over on the orthopaedic side, a fractured leg strung up in 'gallows traction'. In this excruciating attitude he was building a beautiful little model aeroplane, and the reek of balsa cement fought with the antiseptic smell of the ward.

And there was Popsy, propped against several pillows, her colour bluish, her breathing painful to hear. Popsy had a funny heart, Nurse Connell said. They might be able to operate or again they might not. The Chief was to go into it with the heart surgeon when he got back from foreign parts. And meanwhile the Boss Man decreed that Popsy mustn't make the least effort, not even to hold a feeding cup or turn over in bed.

'But maybe you'd be telling her a fairy story,' said Nurse Connell. 'Her head is that full of such things! It isn't nurses and doctors she'd be seeing on the ward, sure 'tis pixies and giants!'

They smiled down at her; and wistfully, hopefully, Popsy smiled back. Fairy story for a little girl who might never grow up, thought Sheila.

Dimly she began to understand what the job would demand of her.

Practical young woman with strong sense of humour. She laughed at something the staff nurse said, and it hurt. She even had to screw up her eyes against the cool spring sunshine as they went out on the balcony. Solarium, Nurse Connell said, was its Sunday name.

There were babies' cots at the far end; but this end was to be her classroom and the children had been waiting and watching for her. Some of them were convalescent, up and about. The others were in their beds which were moved out at nine-thirty every morning.

They sent up a thin cheer when Nurse Velta trotted out with a card-table balanced upside down on her head, set it up and proudly slammed down the jug full of twigs before she hurried back to her linen-sorting. The staff nurse had gone, too. There were beds to be made up and warmed for those three new admissions before she got busy with the theatre cases. Monday was murder. . . .

Sheila unpacked the folding easel, pinned out a big sheet of drawing paper. She felt herself the target for a battery of eager, curious eyes, and she was scared, absolutely tongue-tied. One child had a huge cocoon of bandage round his head, others had an arm or leg in plaster, or a surgical dressing, or just the pallor of long illness. She didn't know how to begin, how to reach them, these small strangers cut off from home and everyday things. The balcony had a view over city roofs, a church spire, a fantastic new block of offices, all cranes and scaffolding and men like toiling ants. Not a tree, not a touch of green wherever her eye rested.

Then her glance fell on the bunch of twigs sticking up, so ungainly, in the jug. She drew in her breath sharply. There is a miracle that happens only with the cherry—and it had happened here and now. In the warmth of this place frail white blossom had burst forth on the leafless, tobacco brown stems. She pointed.

'Look, children. It's spring!'

She took it from there. Words, words . . . They wove a magic spell that dissolved away the dreary rooftop vista, made a host of daffodils dance by the lake and the chaffinch sing on the orchard bough. She taught them verses which they recited together. And then they made pictures in little crayoning books: cherry trees decked like brides, lambs that skipped for the sheer joy of not having a heavy plaster leg and a caliper . . . No muted greens or browns. Spring came to Marbury

General in a riot of glorious technicolor. And how they loved it!

All but Gino. She had noticed him at once: the handsome, pale little boy with the enormous brown eyes. At first, when he refused to join in, she tried coaxing, then gentle scolding, but it was all no use. He just wasn't with them. He played with a length of string tied to his bedhead, twanging it to give a musical note whose tone went up or down as he tightened or slackened the string. Suddenly the string broke and Gino began swearing.

'Damnblasthell. Damnblasthell!'

The others treated it as a joke.

'You want to hear him when he really gets going, miss.'

'He's the organ grinder's monkey, Staff says. Go on, Gino, say some more. Get real mad. Miss, you haven't heard *nothing* yet.'

Sheila had to make a stand, and quickly.

'We're having fun, drawing whatever comes into our heads when we think about spring, and I'm sorry you don't want to join in, Gino. That's up to you! But I can't have you spoiling it for the others. I'm afraid I must ask to have your bed moved back.'

His sudden silence was unnerving. He stared at her unwinkingly, and she had never seen that glare of rage and hatred in a child's eyes before. It made what she'd been trying to do this morning seem poor and futile, miles from reality. She saw his lower lip begin to tremble. He dived down under the bedclothes and stayed there, hiding from them, till the two student nurses came rattling round with elevenses on a trolley and Sheila went off for her coffee break.

Now she suddenly let fly to Dick Sawley.

'It's absurd, isn't it? One small boy of eight taking on the whole world, no holds barred.'

The young doctor pulled a rueful face.

'Absurd but true. Even old Red has given up trying to winkle Gino out of his shell.'

'Well, of course, if *that man* has been bullying the poor little chap. . . .'

'Don't get the wrong idea. This bloke is terrific. He's a man's man. He's been places, had adventures. Once you get him yarning . . . To these kids he's the *most*.' And a hero even to the house physician, Sheila decided resentfully. Dick Sawley hesitated. 'You're new to the hospital set-up. Housemen are just dogsbodies, the nurses carry out their little routine, the consultants pop in and say their piece and pop out again. The real running of the ward is a partnership between Sister and the Registrar. And you can take it from me they make a pretty good job of it.'

'All tiddly and shipshape,' quoted Sheila.

He grinned. 'Everything Bristol fashion.'

'Does the man imagine he's doing his rounds aboard ship?'

'You're bright! I see you've tumbled to it already that old Red was a ship's surgeon before he came to us. He's a thoroughbred mongrel, half doctor, half sailor.'

But she hadn't tumbled to it. This was the most astonishing piece of news she'd had yet.

'But why? From what I've heard he doesn't even *like* children.'

Dick Sawley said: 'Wait till you get really matey and ask him yourself. He came back into the hospital service to widen his experience, I suppose.'

'He gave up an adventurous life at sea for . . .' She made an expressive gesture. 'For Marbury General!'

'I know what you mean. Why not one of the big teaching hospitals? Actually he did three months here under Gannet as a final-year medic, and he seems to have made an impression on the old boy. Landed this job easily because paediatric registrars are so thin on the ground. There's a good reason for that, too. A children's specialist is appointed to a group of hospitals in an area and it narrows down the prospects of reaching consultant grade if kids are your line. It's dicey.'

'Then he must have left the sea for family reasons.' That seemed logical and she looked to Dick Sawley for confirmation. Her remark had put him quite out of countenance.

'Old Red is a bachelor. Though it isn't his fault that he . . .' He floundered, gave it up. Setting down his coffee cup in a hurry, he said: 'Good lord, he'll be along to see his new admissions. I must get cracking on the case-notes. Excuse me.' Off he went with long, loping strides, his stethoscope swinging.

She went back to her class in the solarium, and had to blink, for in this short interval the beds had been rearranged, her easel and little table shoved into a corner. A slim, dark-haired woman in white was giving the children some instructions in a clear, ringing voice. Sheila backed out hastily.

'I beg your pardon, Doctor.'

The woman came after her.

'I'm not a doctor. I'm the physiotherapist. This is the time when I put the children through their breathing exercises. All the theatre cases, you know, so that they take the anaesthetic well. And the asthmas and chests.'

She moved and held herself beautifully. There was an elegance about her, even in an overall, and the smooth dark hair made a perfect setting for pale, clear-cut features. Everything about her caused Sheila to feel young and awkward and untidy. *My hair,* she thought desperately. But at least the physiotherapist was smiling. Evidently Sheila's error flattered her. She was admitting as much when she said lightly: 'The one mistake you must never make is to take a woman doctor for a parent and tell her the ward is closed!'

'Thanks for the tip!'

Just when her confidence was reviving, the next remark took all the stuffing out of her again.

'I had your things moved into that corner so we could space out the beds. And I got an orderly to sweep up your debris—all those bits of crayon. I don't know what

Sister would say if the stuff got trodden into her beautifully oiled floor. The sensible thing to use would be coloured pencils, surely?'

Sheila knew she should have thought of that herself. But she'd brought along just what she happened to have at home until she found out how to set about ordering materials here. She rescued her old attaché case and beat an undignified retreat. *Why* had Dr Gannet to be away? Here she was, blundering round, putting a foot wrong with every step. Perhaps Mr Porson and Mr Mercks had something, after all.

She dumped her stuff, slid into the chair beside Popsy's bed and read her an old-fashioned fairy story in which everyone's wishes came true. The toddlers were getting out of hand, so she spent the rest of the morning at their table, dressing clothes-peg dolls in the scraps of gay material, velvet and lace and ribbon, which her mother always put by when she was sewing.

She was aware of comings and goings in the background. Two children were brought back from the operating theatre and taken into a side-room. A porter trundled through with oxygen cylinders. Nurse Velta, smiling and jolly, no matter how hard-pressed, scurried about bearing blankets and hot water bottles. Trouser-legs were visible below the screens, but no lordly being came striding down the main ward to 'do a round'. And for this small mercy she was truly thankful.

She cut short her lunch in the basement cafeteria, hoping to catch Sister Bain at a quiet moment. But when she tapped at the office door, it turned out to be just another mistake. There sat Sister with her feet up, eating chicken salad off a tray and with a Thermos of coffee beside her. It seemed she always had her lunch like that. It was all hands on deck for the children's dinner, because so many of them needed helping. Then the nurses went off in turns to their meal and Sister had the afternoon, from two to four, leaving one or other of the staff nurses in charge.

'Never mind. Now that you're here, have some coffee.' She handed a cup and gave Sheila a keen but not unfriendly look. 'Trouble?'

Sheila blurted: 'I'm so in the dark. I haven't even a time-table.'

Sister gestured with her fork.

'It will work out. You'll just have to fiddle in your sessions between the nursing attention and special treatments. Mind you, it's tricky. Ilse Devon—she's the superintendent physiotherapist—is busy in her own department most of the time and we never quite know when she'll come up. You must put your heads together.' Between bites of chicken Sister Bain added: 'Some of the children go down to her. Or to be X-rayed. Then there are the doctors' rounds. And visitors. The mums drop in around teatime.'

Tricky? It was like treading a maze.

Ilse Devon. The name seemed to Sheila poised and elegant, like the woman herself. Her goodwill was going to be awfully important. But remembering how her things had been unceremoniously pushed aside to 'space out the beds' for the breathing exercises, the prospect of going into a cosy huddle together over the time-table seemed a bit bleak.

'And then the cases, Sister. I just haven't a clue how much the children are allowed to undertake. I know that a boy who's broken his leg isn't really ill once he's over the shock of the accident, and he may be glad to catch up on his school work and not be a dunce in class. But what about cases like Popsy and Norina?'

'That's up to the Registrar. You need to go down the bed-list with him. I'll mention it this afternoon.'

Well, that wasn't a cheering prospect, either! If only Dr Gannet would hurry back!

She said, as she had said to Dick Sawley: 'Then there's Gino.' Seeing Sister's buttoned-up expression, she leaned forward and said quickly: 'I know. He's difficult. He didn't want to join in what we were doing this morning, but I can't just leave him out, can I?'

Sister Bain set down the tray, brushed off a few crumbs.

'He's the most unco-operative child we ever had. Rude, stubborn . . . Doctor Gannet isn't expecting you to work miracles.'

But miracles happened. She thought of the cherry blossom.

'I could get somewhere with Gino if I knew *why* he's this way. He has lost his parents? Doctor Sawley said something about a foster-mother.'

'He's been brought up by decent, hard-working people, and I feel sorry for them. After all the care they've given him the child shows them no affection whatever. He's just not capable of it. There are such children, you know—shut in on themselves, hostile. They turn into psychiatric cases later on. I'm afraid there's a poor heredity here.' Her face took on a wry expression, as if the story had a nasty taste and would spoil her lunch. 'The father was a musician. He picked this girl up on his travels in Italy and brought her over here. A shiftless sort of life they must have led. Cheap digs wherever he got engagements with his fiddling. They toured in a second-rate variety company and this Victor Cort had a spot near the bottom of the bill. Gipsy music, that sort of thing.'

She made it sound very near the bottom of the bill indeed.

'He must have been doing rather better when they lodged with the Browns in Edgware,' Sister Bain conceded. 'Then the baby came. The mother had always been delicate. Thin and starved-looking. "All eyes," Mrs Brown says. She died at his birth.'

Sheila considered that pathetic odyssey. Engagements so precarious, money tight, fog and dank cold instead of the generous Italian sunshine. Had it broken the girl's spirit? Had she repented often and often of her bargain? Or were they so much in love, these two, that all the hardship seemed worth while? Sister Bain's voice, entirely matter-of-fact, broke into her thoughts.

'He couldn't face up to it. He left his baby with the landlady and cleared out. Typical.'

Typical of a musician? Of a man distracted with grief at his young wife's death?

'The Browns could have put the baby in a Home, but they did the kind and generous thing and brought him up themselves. They moved north—Mr Brown bought a little business. And now they have three children of their own. That woman really has her hands full, looking after the children and helping her husband in the shop, and I believe her when she says Gino has always been difficult, a misfit. He's put us through it, too! Dreadful tantrums. And his language . . . Of course the rheumatism was bad luck. He has had a great deal of pain, and when it was at the worst I've known him scream if someone jogged the bed. And of course there's the risk to the heart. He isn't out of the wood yet.'

'Sister, what's to become of him?'

Sister Bain hesitated, compassion struggling up through her annoyance and dislike.

'You can be sure the almoner will do her best. She'll get him in somewhere.'

Sheila said incredulously: 'You mean the Browns don't want him back?'

'Look, Miss Thorne, it was one of those unofficial arrangements that are frowned on. They never had a penny towards his keep, and the child hasn't even rewarded them with love. He behaved disgracefully the last time Mrs Brown came.' She tightened her lips. 'If I'd had my way he'd have been isolated from the other children for a few days to teach him a lesson, but I was overruled.'

By Dr Gannet, Sheila felt sure. He was humane and wise. Conscience gave her a twinge. She had threatened Gino with the very same punishment this morning! As she prepared for the afternoon, she wrestled with the puzzle. The Browns had been so kind. Even heroically kind. And the thing just hadn't worked out. Why? *Why?* At some point along the line a baby who had known no other home, no other parents, had been turned into a stubborn little rebel, all knotted up inside with hate and suspicion. Well, Sheila thought, I can be stubborn, too.

She found the solarium barred to her again. The children were having their afternoon rest. The toddlers in the main ward, who had been playing, squabbling, begging to be carried about and nursed, were at bed-rest, too, lying in their cots like so many little wax dolls. The quiet was unnerving!

Sheila went to help Stephen with his model of a jet plane. They got balsa cement on the sheet and she hoped to goodness they could get it off with nail varnish remover before Sister was on their track. But it wasn't Sister Bain who appeared at the bedside, it was Ilse Devon. Her laugh was edgy.

' Sorry, Miss Thorne. We do seem to tread on one another's heels, don't we? I want to put Stephen through his active and passive movements.'

Kneeling at the bedside, her face flushed and her hair tumbling over her cheek, Sheila squinted up at her through the cords and pulleys.

' You've caught us at a tricky moment. If we could just fix this strut . . . It'll only take two ticks, the cement dries like magic.'

The physiotherapist turned away sharply with no comment. Sheila saw her go to another orthopaedic case and draw the screens round.

They fixed the strut and Stephen admired their handiwork.

' Oh, boy, isn't she smashing? I bet she has a smart turn of speed, too. Tomorrow we'll launch her.'

Sheila's lip twitched. Ship talk, and she could guess where he'd learnt it. In the boy's pleasure she felt her own hopes take wing. This was what she was here for. Call it lessons or play or what you liked, it just meant giving every child in this ward a dream for tomorrow.

One of the nurses who had paused to admire the plane said she had some solvent in the cloakroom and many were the times she'd had to use it in a hurry, because nail varnish was forbidden on ward duty. Sheila would find it in a carrier bag under the cardigan you daren't let Sister catch you wearing and the knitting you never had time for, anyway. She was nipping back with the stuff when, on the short corridor and without any warning at all, she came face to face with her ogre.

'Miss Thorne?'

He planted himself in her path: a tall, broad-shouldered man with a tough, weathered look and intensely blue eyes. Old Red! She felt tricked, for he wasn't old at all. He could be thirty or thereabouts. He had a head of splendid dark coppery hair that would have been a woman's pride and glory. In him, it was a battle flag.

He wasted no time. In the crisp tone of authority that would have told her who he was, even if she hadn't guessed already, he said:

'I'm Doctor Gannet's Registrar, and in his absence I'm in charge of the unit. I want to make one thing quite clear, whatever ideas the Chief himself may have about your work. Treatments come first. Any distractions you find for the children must be fitted in without disorganizing the real work of the ward. Is that understood? Mrs Devon has had to complain to me that a boy missed his session of massage today because you refused to interrupt some game.'

So Ilse wasn't Miss but Mrs Devon. Even as she noted that fact, furious colour rushed up into her cheeks. Her eyes blazed away at him.

'Stephen and I kept Mrs Devon waiting only two minutes. I'm sorry she took offence. It was the very last thing I intended.' She choked. 'I've made mistakes. It's been that kind of day. But don't you think you might have the courtesy to hear both sides before you judge a case?'

The instant it was out she wished it back. Dick Sawley made a hero of him, the harassed nurses submitted to his bullying, Sister Bain had dropped her a plain hint that it was wise to 'keep on the right side of him'. She remembered all that—now, when it was too late. She was conscious of actual physical fear; of trembling knees, a dry throat, a face from which every vestige of colour had drained away.

She was saved by Sister Bain who came hurrying up.

'Oh, Doctor Redfern, I'm glad I've caught you. I came back early because I'm so worried about this pneumonia. The new case. In spite of the oxygen . . .'

The Registrar turned on his heel and they went back into the ward, Sister Bain talking earnestly as she kept up with his long stride.

It took all the courage in the world to follow them, to see this frustrating, shattering day to its end.

She removed the stiff patch of balsa cement from Stephen's sheet and spent half an hour at the doll's dressmaking with the little ones. Then she heard the children out on the balcony read aloud in turn till school was over at teatime, when the visitors came in.

Gino had burrowed under the bedclothes when it was his turn to read. She went on to the next child without any comment. He cautiously surfaced and found the new piece of string she had tied firmly to the bedhead, and after a minute or two he began softly twanging the string.

That was one little thing salvaged from the day. She had made a beginning with Gino. She knew already in her heart that no matter what grand schemes Dr Gannet had in mind for her, the job would stand or fall by what she achieved with one lonely small boy who was so sure the whole world was against him.

It was raining heavily when she left for home: a

sudden, torrential downpour out of a doom-threatening sky. In the eerie half-light she paused on the steps of the porter's lodge to tie a rain-hood over her hair.

A long silver and black Jaguar nosed its way out of the hospital yard and halted under the archway. The entrance light glinted on the coppery hair of the man in the driving seat. He seemed to be leaning towards her, smiling in her direction.

He was offering her a lift. Flag of truce, she thought.

She still burned with resentment at the things he had said and the tone in which he had said them. But she'd get nowhere without his goodwill. And it was ridiculous to get drenched to the skin, out of foolish pride. . . . Even as she hesitated she felt a stirring of excitement, a queer little sense of elation and pleasure. Perhaps he wasn't such an ogre. Perhaps she was like Popsy, who saw pixies and giants instead of ordinary, busy human beings!

Ilse Devon came running down the steps past her and Dr Redfern leaned right across and held open the car door. As she slid in beside him, Sheila heard her say in a gay, lilting voice: ' Red darling, what a wonderful surprise! Just when I was going to blue my all on a taxi. . . .'

The long, swift-looking car moved into the stream of evening traffic. And Sheila began plodding through the puddles to the bus stop.

So that's how it is, she thought. Now I know everything.

And somehow this last surprise was the bitterest of all.

CHAPTER II

Dr Timothy Redfern. The name leapt out at her from the In-and-Out board in the entrance hall of the main building where the doctors were grouped under headings:

Surgeons, Physicians, Registrars, Anaesthetists. Dick Sawley's name was not in the list and she decided there must be a separate indicator for 'other ranks'. Certainly someone had done a beautiful job with gold and black lettering on the polished mahogany board and it gave her ideas. Why shouldn't *I love Elvis* be set out just as handsomely above the bedhead of a teenager with time on her hands?

Hastily she added 'Small pot gold paint' to the list she had sat up so late preparing last night. She was on her way to deliver it at the hospital secretary's office. He was a grey, precise little man whom she'd met already at her interview, and now he glanced doubtfully through the list and said he would take it up with the education people. Peering at her over his spectacles, he remarked that though her salary had been agreed between M.G.H. and the education authority, they were still arguing how and by whom her materials were to be paid for.

'Of course it's all laid down in the Act, but certain things are—um—left to the discretion of the employing authority.'

'They are?' said Sheila, mystified.

'You see, my dear young lady, the Education Act of 1944 empowers local education authorities to—um—make special arrangements for children or young people who by reason of any extraordinary circumstances are unable to attend a suitable school.'

He paused to let this sink in, and Sheila remarked that pneumonia or a broken leg might well seem to be extraordinary circumstances.

'Quite, quite. Many authorities use their powers under the Act to—um—provide the services of a teacher where a hospital has no special school attached. And it is laid down in the Act that though the salary of any such teacher is not covered by the Burnham Reports, he or she shall—um—receive adequate remuneration. But in the matter of books and teaching aids and '—his eye rapidly travelled down Sheila's list again—'little pots of gold paint . . . Dear me!'

'That was just an idea I had,' Sheila faltered. 'I'll cross it off.'

'Allow me.' He whisked a biro out of his pocket and neatly deleted the small pot of gold paint. 'The trouble is, you see, this sort of thing has been on a voluntary basis at M.G.H. till now.'

'Oh, I do understand that.'

'Our good friend Miss Furlong would bring along two or three books from the municipal library and read to the children.'

'It was sweet and kind of her,' said Sheila quickly. 'But Doctor Gannet——'

'I know, my dear young lady, I know.' He glanced down the list a third time, his biro hovering, like an auctioneer's hammer. Going, going, gone. 'I must warn you it all takes time. I shall have your list typed out and put it up to them. Let us keep our fingers crossed.' And our biro in our pocket, thought Sheila. 'And in the meantime, my advice is—um—if you're wise you'll improvise.'

If you're wise you'll improvise. It jigged in her head like a nonsense rhyme. *Practical young woman with strong sense of humour* began to sound a bit corny, too. This job would send you up the wall if you weren't absolutely determined to see every obstacle as a challenge.

They seemed to have moved all the beds round, and she had to run about looking for the bored little boy who wanted a new jigsaw, because he had done the old one so many times he turned the bits of puzzle over to the plain side and put it together that way to make it harder. She was hoping Stephen's plane was ready for the ceremonial take-off, but as she approached his bed Sister hove in sight and told her not to bother him today, he 'wasn't up to it'. She saw Dr Sawley and a nurse busy with his weights and pulleys, and it gave her a sick feeling.

But at least she got a smile of welcome from Norina, who was tickled pink with the idea of doing *I love Elvis* quite beautifully in the middle of a large white card, the back of an old calendar—if you're wise you'll improvise—and designing a border of flowers. Sheila drew out the lettering for her, gave her a box of coloured pencils and left her to it.

For the children on the balcony she meant to suggest writing letters home, first in rough, then copying them out neatly on some jolly notepaper she had dug up, and enclosing the pictures they had done yesterday. That rather left Gino out, and she racked her brain for something he would enjoy doing besides twanging a length of string.

She had to pass Popsy's bed and saw that her mother was there—a well-dressed, haggard woman involved with some knitting, her eyes raised from the work every moment or two in an anxious look at the child.

'Is it a cardigan for Popsy?' said Sheila, as she passed by. 'How pretty!'

She was a few yards from the bed when the woman impulsively jumped up and came after her.

'Could I have a word with you, please? Are you a doctor?'

'I'm the ward teacher. If you'd like to read aloud to Popsy, I have a book of fairy stories. I know she'd love that.'

The woman didn't seem to listen. She lowered her voice and said urgently: 'Do help me. We're so dreadfully worried about our little girl. Sister says I can come in and sit with her whenever I like, though it isn't easy to manage, you know. But she's so busy, she hasn't time to tell me anything. No one tells me anything. And they seem to hustle you out when the doctors come round.'

Sheila felt a twinge of sympathy. She knew exactly how it was.

'I'm new here, I can't really help you, I'm afraid.

Perhaps, if you wait till Sister has a spare moment——'

That was the magic word. How often she had heard it already! 'If you can spare a moment——'

Popsy's mother gave a discouraged sigh. 'It would be such a comfort if we knew what they were doing for her.'

Sheila hesitated. 'They're waiting till Doctor Gannet gets back from Switzerland.'

'You mean they're doing *nothing*?'

'She's just resting. She hasn't to make the least effort. She's really in very good care, you know.'

The woman turned away, her face working. Sheila's heart ached for her. But she had to put on her 'shining morning face' to greet the children on the balcony. They were eager to see her and ready for mischief.

Jackie trotted after her like Mary's little lamb. She let him hand out the writing paper while someone else sharpened the pencils in a gadget like a tiny mincing machine clamped to the table. They'd have played with that for hours till the pencils were reduced to stubs and shavings. They weren't half so keen on the letter-writing!

They were living in a new world, the fantastic world of a hospital, and they couldn't put it into words. One little girl wrote furiously, her tongue following the words; a boy with his right arm in plaster printed out the words in shaky capitals with the left hand, and made it the shortest letter on record. DEAR MUM THIS IS FROM YOUR LOVING BOY FRED. Another child was worried about what was happening to his hamsters. 'When they curl up they aren't dead they are having bedrest like me please love them twice a day.' One child sucked his pencil, staring glumly at the blank sheet, then suddenly began to cover the paper with little people.

'This is Matron, miss.' He had made her very thin and tall with a sort of heron's plume. Sister Bain was round as a dumpling. He asked for coloured pencils and gave her bright red cheeks. Then he used the same red pencil for the hair of a giant with he-man shoulders. Sheila didn't have to ask who that was. 'But who's this?' A figure in a short skirt, a thick fringe of hair over the eyes and an enormous smile like a slice of melon, who appeared to be offering a bunch of flowers to the red-haired giant. The child went all tonguetied and covered the picture with his hand.

I must do something about my hair, Sheila thought, amused and oddly embarrassed. But I surely don't go about grinning like a Cheshire cat! As for handing bouquets to the Registrar . . .

She had to skip coffee break because one of the student nurses popped in with a message. She was wanted in Dr Gannet's room. 'Across in Outpatients. It's the first door past the lift. You just knock and walk in.'

Marbury General was proud of its new Outpatient department. Instead of a drab waiting hall with hard benches there was a modern décor, little tables round which stood comfortable chairs, a receptionist with flowers on her desk and a supply of bright magazines, a snack-bar in one corner. The names of doctors and surgeons were on doors opening off the hall. Each had a suite consisting of consulting room and examination cubicle. The whole place was as busy as a railway station: nurses and secretaries popping in and out of doors, porters with stretchers and wheelchairs, patients going for snacks or jumping up and bolting into a doctor's room as their names were called.

Her head whirling with all this, Sheila found Dr Gannet's room, knocked and walked in, her hopes high and her step confident. If the Chief, returning from the Swiss congress earlier than expected, sent for her straight away before even 'seeing his beds', it could only be because he was bursting with ideas about their wonderful partnership, whose aim was to prevent any child feeling cut off from home or hopelessly behind in his school work after a stay in Marbury General.

But the Chief wasn't back. It was Dr Timothy

Redfern she found sitting in Dr Gannet's chair at Dr Gannet's desk, with the filing cabinet open and X-ray films and charts spread out before him. And even in that sickening moment of let-down, the thought crossed her mind that he looked every inch a consultant. The well-cut dark suit, the fine physique, that air of authority. . . .

Why had he sent for her? There had been no clash with Ilse Devon this morning, for she hadn't appeared on the ward. Well then? She braced herself, facing him across the desk.

Red was squinting at an X-ray film which he held up to the light. He put it back in the big black envelope and returned a case-card to its proper place in the files. And he wasn't keeping her waiting just for show-off, Sheila realized suddenly. He was blazingly angry and he was putting himself under restraint. He needed time. Was that something a man acquired at sea, like the passion for neatness—because when the cramped quarters of a ship formed your world everything had to be organized down to the last detail?

He straightened up, motioned her to the chair opposite, and said in an even voice whose quietness was somehow more formidable than yesterday's annoyed outburst: 'You accused me of not hearing both sides, Miss Thorne. But in this case there aren't two sides. You spoke out of turn, and there's no knowing where such a thing may end.'

Sheila gave him a level look.

'I simply have no idea what you're talking about.'

He made a movement of furious impatience, though he still had his voice under control.

'Now look. A mother goes to the admin office and asks to see the Medical Superintendent of the hospital. When they press her for the reason she goes all to pieces—as it happens, she's a neurotic, difficult person and she's been through a lot of anxiety. She tells them she has a child here, hovering between life and death. And nothing is being done for her. Not a thing. The ward teacher has told her it's all held up till Doctor Gannet returns from a fancy holiday in the Alps.'

'Popsy's mother,' whispered Sheila.

She didn't know how deathly pale she had gone. She only knew she felt so faint and sick, she had to hold on to the edge of the desk for support. Red didn't help her. He merely waited. And his eyes, bright blue and angry, seemed to her pitiless. At that moment she had no pride left and her hopes were in the dust.

When she could make words come she said: 'I was sorry for her. No one had time to tell her anything. I said the big decision had to wait till Doctor Gannet was back; that's *all* I said. She'd asked what treatment Popsy was receiving.'

Red made a sharp gesture, then slowly clenched up his hand.

'The only treatment for an atrial septal defect—a hole in the heart—is operation. And before the surgeon takes that on, he and Doctor Gannet will have to consider the results of the tests we're carrying out now.' He made one of those abrupt gestures towards the big black envelope and the cardiographs which looked like recordings of earth tremors. 'The mother got it all wrong. Granted. But then you had no business to tell her anything. It was a gross breach of etiquette to give an opinion on a case.'

The last spark of pride made Sheila exclaim: 'But I never——'

She didn't finish it. The feverish thought came to her that when she stood up to Red yesterday he had decided there and then to get rid of her at the first opportunity— and she had handed it to him on a plate! She heard her own voice, quite flat and dead and coming from a long distance.

'I meant to be kind and I've made an awful mess of it. I'm sorry, truly sorry. I know that doesn't make any difference, because you——'

Her voice trailed off. She stood up.

'Because I what?' Red demanded.

'Because you think I'm a trouble-maker and you don't want me on the Children's Ward.'

A pause that seemed to confirm her worst fears. But when he spoke he sounded embarrassed rather than angry.

'Anyone can make a blunder. But it isn't everyone who honestly accepts the blame.' Sheila got the idea a strict sense of fairness was struggling in him with all sorts of other feelings. 'As for your job——'

He motioned to the chair, and Sheila found herself meekly sitting down again while he prowled up and down, jerking his remarks at her as if he had made up his mind to match her honesty with equal frankness.

'Gannet springs these things on us. No sooner do we get the unit organized than he's off on another tack and we're at sixes and sevens again.' He ran an irritable hand through his hair. 'We'll be lucky if he doesn't come back from this blasted congress brimful of ideas to close the ward and organize us into a domiciliary team to run round treating the kids at home!'

The rueful grin which accompanied this remark turned Sheila's ogre quite suddenly into a harassed human being with a load of responsibility on his shoulders. He ought to be used to it! A young doctor who went to be a ship's surgeon must find it unnerving to have in his hands the lives of all who sailed in her, in all sorts of critical emergencies, and without the hospital set-up and the authority of his Chief behind him. He must feel, Sheila thought with an unexpected twinge of sympathy, very much as she did at Marbury General!

She took her courage in both hands. 'I'm all at sea in this place and I think I need your help. So far it's been mostly play. For instance, I helped Stephen with his model plane. He was hoping to fly it today.'

His mouth went down. 'Not a hope. I've just been ordering up the mobile X-ray outfit. He has pain and tension under the plaster, and I'm afraid it may be an abscess.'

'Oh, what wretched luck,' faltered Sheila. She gave Red a searching look. 'But it's only a temporary setback, isn't it? I'm hoping to do some real work with Stephen. You see, he's due to take an important examination in a few months, and even an hour or two slogging away together every day, and some quiet reading on his own, would help him not to forget too much. Perhaps his school would send along the books he needs.' She made a wry little face. 'I only hope it won't be quite beyond me! I've been teaching in a junior school, you know, and I expect I'll have to sit up late at night to keep one lesson ahead of Stephen. But please don't tell Mr Porson!'

There had been amusement in his face. Suddenly the smile was gone; his eyes seemed to become bluer, more piercing.

'What has Mr Porson to do with it?'

'Nothing,' Sheila said quickly, with a panic feeling that she was tottering on the brink of another breach of etiquette. She added lamely: 'I don't think his ideas are quite as advanced as Doctor Gannet's.'

Red was still looking at her very hard, as if he suspected a double meaning and resented it furiously.

'My ideas aren't all that advanced, either,' he said bluntly. 'I can tell you this. You'll be a lot more popular with Stephen if you stick to model planes.'

Sheila persisted. 'That's fun, but it won't exercise his *mind*. He'll never have such a good chance again to get through some solid reading. Lying in bed is fine for that. Didn't R. L. S. say, "I work best in a recumbent posture"?'

Red looked taken aback only for a moment. Then he grinned appreciatively.

'Come to think of it, Byron said, "Gin and water is the whole of my inspiration." You won't get me over to your side, Miss Thorne! I contend that a bright lad like Stephen will catch up on his school work soon enough.'

'But please won't you see, it's just because he's so bright that he could take some real work in his stride now.'

'So the poor kid gets no peace even while he's laid up! He has my sympathy. I may as well admit I hated school myself, and every time the exams came round I dreamt of running away to sea.'

Sickeningly let down—because he couldn't have made it plainer that she was not to count on him as an ally—Sheila said: 'Well, you got your wish in the end.'

'Yes,' said Red.

But into that one word he packed so much bitterness, such haunting regret, that Sheila's heart twisted with pity. She pulled herself up sharp. Why should she feel sorry for him? He had gone to sea, fulfilling his boyhood dream. And then he had thrown it over and come back into the hospital service, for reasons of his own. She had begun to guess at those reasons ever since she saw Ilse Devon drive off with him last night, heard the caress in her voice. *Red darling, what a wonderful surprise!*

That wasn't her business. What there was between these two didn't interest her in the slightest. But the memory caused her an agonizing shyness; she actually felt her cheeks burn and had to avoid his eyes. She went on talking very fast about her plans. The handwork and hobbies—he mustn't think it was to be all 'set lessons'.

'And music, of course. I'm hoping to get at Gino that way.'

'You won't get anywhere with Gino. We've all tried.' As she said nothing, he frowned. 'Look, the father was a vagabond musician, the boy plays for hours with a piece of string. That suggests to you he's a musical genius?' he asked with heavy sarcasm.

He made her so *mad*!

'Of course not, Doctor. But there must be some way of reaching that child, and I shall find it.'

'Good luck to you.' The phone rang, and as he

reached for it he said: ' By the way, that string tied to the bed. It's a stranded lady. Granny on a reef.'

' I didn't know I was expected to teach them sailor's knots,' said Sheila coldly. ' It's all laid down in the Act, I suppose.'

That sent his eyebrows up.

On the telephone he heard the secretary of Hamish Dee, their orthopaedic surgeon, announcing that Mr Dee had been called into consultation urgently and wouldn't be at the General this morning.

' He'll try to make it this afternoon. I'm sorry. I know your people will have everything laid on already.'

' No trouble at all. Keep them on their toes,' said Dr Redfern. ' Like boat drill.'

He was being sarcastic again. It was a habit he'd got into for self-defence against the endless frustrations of this job. But the girl wasn't to know that. She sounded shocked as she said good morning and rang off.

What a bully he is, thought Sheila. She had been able to hear both voices quite distinctly, and she suddenly bolted from the room before he could stop her.

She couldn't remember ever going through so many emotions in ten minutes, and at the end of it she was left with a feeling of helpless fury. Even with Dr Gannet to back her up, she'd be blocked at every turn by the Registrar. She was being paid to do a job with which he seemed to have no sympathy at all. And he was quite sure she would fail with Gino. Keep on the right side of him, Sister Bain had advised. Well, she had tried.

From now on, it's war, she told herself, and trudged back to the unit, where she was greeted by ' Music While You Work ' at full blast, and the children squealing delightedly because a small boy, due for the doctor's visit, was scrambling about under the beds with two nurses in pursuit.

In Dr Gannet's room, Timothy Redfern put down the phone and scowled ferociously at it. Another day gone haywire. Hamish Dee's round put off to this afternoon.

Young Stephen's leg giving trouble. It would be a case of having him into the theatre, cutting down the plaster cast and draining the abscess. It had been a strain trying to bring Popsy's mother round to a reasonable frame of mind and without losing his own temper in the process. Then his interview with the Thorne girl.

Sister had asked him to go through the bed-list with her, and somehow or other they hadn't got down to it. They had started arguing and he wasn't at all sure he'd come out best. She was stubborn and she had spirit. Most women never really knew their own minds. He'd call that the curse of Eve. His eyes went bleak as he thought what it had meant in his own life. But this Sheila Thorne knew exactly where she was going.

He was remembering that when she argued a point, her whole body seemed to take part in it. The hands made expressive gestures, the eyes held a flame.

Suddenly he chuckled. 'It's all laid down in the Act.' That was old Farrell in the admin office, of course. But she hadn't meant it as a shared joke. She'd been warning him off—like a robin defending its own corner of the garden. The smile reached his eyes. Five foot two of slim young womanhood challenging his authority!

'Good luck to you!' he said aloud softly. And this time he meant it.

CHAPTER III

Sheila saw a consultant's round for the first time that afternoon. 'The Admiral is to be piped aboard at six bells,' was how Dr Sawley put it, appearing after lunch in a clean white coat and with his hair sleeked down.

Sheila saw the point. There was someone who would revel in all this pomp and circumstance. But it wasn't Sister, whose free time had gone for a burton with the change in Mr Dee's plans. Or the nurses who had to spruce up the ward and get all the children into bed, washed and tidy, for the second time that day. One nurse was detailed to help Dr Sawley with a sort of complicated puzzle, setting out case-notes and charts and X-rays on a table in the centre of the ward. Even Sheila got involved in the scurrying round. 'I'll be grateful if you can find them something quiet to do, Miss Thorne,' Sister Bain said, adding with one of her funny looks: 'No chalks or balsa cement, *please!*' Nothing missed her eagle eye, it seemed!

The trouble was, orthopaedic cases didn't want 'something quiet to do'. They were bursting with energy. 'My legs are all prancy and dancy,' confided one little boy with an arm extended on a long splint. He ran a toy car up and down the splint, making Z-car noises, till Sister corked him up with a piece of barley sugar.

When Sheila went to the store-room to dig in her cupboard for more drawing paper, she found Nurse Velta posted as a look-out. Nurse Connell had instructed her to 'cut the bread and butter with one eye and listen for Mr Dee with the other', and presently her shrill summons: 'Sister ma'am, Mr Dee done make his walk!' brought Sister hurrying from her office, while Sheila, amused and a little scornful, peeped from the store-room to see the procession enter the ward.

Hamish Dee—a shaggy, sandy, thick-set man who didn't look to her in the least like a consultant—was attended by his own secretary and surgical officer, and the honours of the ward were done by Dr Redfern and the houseman with Sister and a couple of nurses in solid support. Sheila saw an agitated whispering going on in the rear. A slip-up after all these elaborate preparations. A plump nurse in mauve stripes was sent hastily to the telephone.

Sheila hadn't seen her before. Presumably she'd been off duty yesterday. She spoke into the phone in a hoity-toity voice to which Sheila took an instant dislike.

'Physiotherapy? This is Kids. We omitted to let Mrs Devon know that . . . Oh, she's on her way?' She clamped the receiver down ill-humouredly and spoke to Sheila. 'Sister has me haring round. Afraid the physios will miss something! She might have known Red would pass on the word. Naturally.'

Naturally. If hospital etiquette didn't permit a registrar and a 'physio' to lunch together, Sheila supposed they would contrive to snatch the odd moment. Then she felt uncomfortable. The idea seemed all wrong for someone as direct and forthright as Timothy Redfern.

At that moment Ilse Devon appeared. Sheila had been quite certain, after what happened yesterday, that Ilse looked on her as a disturber of the peace, a troublesome intruder; and now the friendliness of her greeting took her by surprise. She saw her hovering there with her books and papers. 'Dodgy, isn't it, once the procession has started.' And she murmured: 'How beautiful they are, the lordly ones. . . .' with a fine edge of scorn on her voice.

'Mine is a dodgy sort of job, I find,' Sheila said with feeling.

Ilse Devon gave her a quick glance, considered a moment.

'Look, if you're not in a special hurry to get home, how about coming down for a cuppa after school? I'll show you the department and put you in the picture about my ward visits.'

Sheila was very pleased, and showed it. She needed friends—especially since she'd realized she mustn't count on the Registrar's backing. And it would be fine to get things sorted out with Mrs Devon so that they weren't 'treading on one another's heels', as Ilse herself had put it.

'How kind!' she exclaimed. 'I'll come down. It will be about half-past four.'

A nod and a smile and Ilse Devon slipped into the

ward, joining the doctors at the bedside of the first child they had to see.

'That's right. Dig yourself well in,' said a voice at Sheila's elbow. Mauve Stripes was giving her a knowing wink.

Sheila resented both the tone and the wink.

'I know Mrs Devon is very busy. It's good of her to spare time to show me round.'

The staff nurse chanted: 'Will you walk into my parlour, said the spider to the fly.' Again the wink. 'Get it? Spider. Black widow. Something pretty deadly, too. Well, dear, don't say I didn't warn you.'

It sank in. 'Mrs Devon is a widow?'

'Not permanently.' She had puffy features and small eyes beady with malice. 'It's ever so romantic. Fate doesn't often give a woman the chance to rub out her mistakes and start again from scratch.'

What was the girl getting at—with her mysterious hints and winks? There was more to come, lots more. But though a painful curiosity burned in her, Sheila knew she mustn't listen. It was fatal to listen to gossip.

She said hastily: 'I'm going to nip across to the solarium before those children start a fight or something. I'll follow you in, Staff. Do you mind?' She softened this by adding: 'I hope I've got it right: mauve stripes and a belt with a silver buckle does mean a staff nurse?'

'It does, too.' She perked up. 'I'm Porson. My uncle is on the Management Committee.'

She said it with pride and complacency. If she knew what Sheila thought about that uncle of hers! Now that she knew they were related, she could see the likeness. It was in the heavy features, the set of the eyes with their light lashes and the eyebrows that were just a bony ridge.

Nurse Porson chatted on: 'Uncle Joe is going to stand for the City Council at the May elections. He'll be an alderman one day. Just you wait. And I daresay he'll get to be Lord Mayor.' Perhaps she saw the amusement Sheila couldn't hide, for she added in a crafty tone: ' He's just the man they need in public affairs. He's out to save the ratepayers' money and he has a real nose for scandal. Wherever he finds it, he'll bring it out into the open. If there were more good citizens like Uncle Joe——'

All sorts of warning bells rang in Sheila's mind. Staff Nurse Porson might perform her ward duties admirably, but as the eyes and ears of that upright citizen, Uncle Joe, she was a menace around this place. Just supposing you were vulnerable; supposing there was something in your life that you wished to keep private, a mistake you were trying to live down. . . .

Nurse Porson drew in a breath over her teeth with a juicy sound. ' Between you and me and the gate-post——'

Sheila blurted: ' I can hear somebody calling "Nurse".'

It worked. The staff nurse scuttled off. Actually it wasn't Sister on the warpath, but a child whose teddy-bear had got stuck fast between the cot bars—but Nurse Porson hadn't waited to hear that!

Sheila rescued the teddy-bear herself, and then she had to put on a big hankie as a bandage before the child was satisfied. The delay was unlucky. Mr Dee's procession was just coming past, and there she was, trapped. She stood near the wall and tried to make herself invisible, but Mr Dee's eye was caught by the comical spectacle of the solemn little boy and the teddy-bear with unwinking stare, side by side in the cot and both with enormous head bandages. He made some remark and the people round him laughed heartily. It was a brave man who didn't find a consultant's little jokes funny!

But Red wasn't laughing. He looked impatient and annoyed, and after that one swift glance at him, Sheila daren't look up again. All the same, it brought back her resentment with a rush. He was annoyed because she had slowed down the great man's progress round the ward—by precisely one minute!—and perhaps he even thought she had deliberately sought the limelight. Or perhaps, she thought bitterly, he wasn't satisfied with her spica. He'd already complained about the knots she tied! I just can't do right for him, she summed it up.

A nurse who must, Sheila felt sure, have nautical forebears, had tidied the solarium, whisking out of sight every scrap of paper—including the children's half-finished letters home—and Gino's fiddle string. Sheila felt like 'creating', but for once Gino didn't. He lay quiet, fixing fever-bright eyes on the bit of the main ward he could see when someone came in or out. Almost automatically Sheila bent to straighten his molehill of bedclothes in passing, and a small hand, hot and dry, grabbed hers and held on tight.

He spoke in a whisper out of the corner of his mouth, like an old lag. 'Are they cutting Stephen's leg off?'

She cast a startled glance into the ward, where the orthopaedic team had reached Stephen's bed—like a monkeys' playground it looked from this distance—and Mr Dee had suddenly taken off his jacket and handed it to a nurse.

'Good gracious, no! What gave you such an idea?'

'Doctor Red said it.' And that made it gospel to one little boy whose faith in grown-ups had had some hard knocks. 'He said: "It's tough luck, but we'll have to cut it down."'

'The plaster, silly. Not the leg!' The fantastic things that went on in a child's mind! They had all been so sure that he couldn't be reached, that his thoughts were all turned inward. And here he was worrying himself sick over Stephen's leg. She held his eyes steadily. 'Not to worry. Stephen's going to be all right. And tomorrow——'

Tomorrow he'll be flying his plane. She stopped herself just in time. Who was she to make any such promise—she, with no medical knowledge whatever? She thought of Popsy's mother. That still made her feel so awful.

There was just the fractional pause, then she went on smoothly: 'Tomorrow I'll bring along my guitar and we'll have some music. Will you like that?'

But somehow it was the wrong thing to say; the frightening thing. He pulled his hand away. And though he didn't dive under the bedclothes, he shut his eyes tight, and that was a way of hiding, too. He wanted nothing to do with her or her music.

She began rooting about for the children's letters. They were in the waste paper basket, and she saw why. When her eye wasn't on them, the little wretches had had a glorious game of paper darts.

'Never mind.' She kept her voice bright and cheerful, though she was shaking with anger inside. 'Jackie will bring them round. Each of you pick out your own and try to smooth it out. It'll be such a lovely surprise for them at home, we're going to send them off—even if they *are* a bit crumpled. I've got envelopes and stamps here and there's a mailing box in the entrance hall. Now I want the envelopes very neat indeed——'

That really got them, they made the most heroic efforts to smooth out the worst creases, even if it meant smudging those laborious masterpieces in technicolor.

'My lamb has gone green. Oh, miss, can't I do it again?'

'There wouldn't be time. School is nearly over.' If she weakened, they'd learn nothing from this at all. 'But the next letters we write home will be so beautiful, your parents will want to keep them *always*.'

Red's hair had run in the wash, and Sister Bain's rosy cheeks seemed smeared with tears. But the rows and rows of crosses at the end of each letter were what mattered. If my little boy wrote to me from hospital, thought Sheila . . . She was suddenly aware that Gino's eyes were open, he was watching every movement. And when she said goodbye to the children and went off with a handful of letters to post, his eyes followed her as if he didn't want to let her go.

❖   ❖   ❖

Ilse Devon was quite something when she came on the ward, but in her own department she was undisputed queen. She had several assistants, and Sheila was in time to see them at work, giving wax baths or electric treatment for rheumatism or helping fracture cases, who had come back as outpatients, to bring an injured limb into full use.

'I'd simply no idea all this went on,' Sheila confessed.

'No one has any idea! If every minute is precious when I come up to the unit, now you know why. I like to do the children's work myself as far as possible. It takes time to win their confidence, and the same person should give the treatment regularly.'

That was absolutely true. But anyone would be blind who imagined that was the only reason why Mrs Devon liked to come up to the Children's Ward, thought Sheila. She had been shown over the department and now they were having a cuppa in the superintendent's room which was decorated in a striking scheme of lime green and a soft red. Sheila felt sure Ilse had designed it herself, it made such a perfect background for her glossy dark hair and creamy skin. Yes, she could look superbly elegant in a white coat—and in her office! As an afterthought, the effect on patients she interviewed here must be to jerk them right out of their aches and pains and offer them the challenge of radiant wellbeing.

Even the tea-things were a personal choice, not the plain hospital ware with MGH for a decoration. They sipped and talked. Sheila felt her shyness fall away. Ilse listened so sympathetically to her problems that it was like a sudden cold shower when she said: 'Forgive me, but isn't this rather a dead-end job for you? I mean, I should have thought it would appeal to someone older.'

Sheila managed to smile. 'I just don't know how someone older would cope!'

'Experience counts for something, surely? And by someone older, perhaps I just mean someone unambitious.' As she spoke she leaned forward with a smile of such friendliness that Sheila couldn't believe she meant her words to be so cruel. 'I'm not prying. I'm sure you have your reasons.' Her brows went up in a smiling question. 'My guess is that you're not worrying about promotion and salary scales because you're going to throw it all up and get married, anyway!'

Sheila said hastily and with vehemence: 'Oh, no! Nothing like that.'

The other woman insisted smilingly: 'Not even a steady boy-friend? I can't believe it.'

Sheila set down her cup with a little clatter. 'It happens to be true. I'm much too busy to bother with boy-friends. Steady or unsteady!'

They both laughed. But it wasn't much of a joke really, Sheila thought. It wasn't even a consultant's joke! Mrs Devon always had the advantage, she could make her feel young—young and foolish. The reason she had come to Marbury General was her own business; she was suddenly quite determined not to mention her father's illness and have Ilse Devon looking on this thing as a sacrifice.

'Oh, well,' said Ilse, 'sooner or later you'll change your mind!' And suddenly she was quite serious, a strange haunted look in her eyes. 'Surely it's every woman's dream to put her life in the hands of a fine man. A man she can depend on and trust to the ends of the earth.'

Sheila said nothing. She felt horribly embarrassed. Ilse Devon had lost a little of her poise and her hands were nervously busy with the tea-things. She exclaimed: 'Hamish Dee coming in so late has thrown us all out of gear! What did you think of him? I hope you were impressed?'

'Tremendously,' said Sheila, then hesitated. 'Though he doesn't *look* like a consultant, however clever he is really! When he was walking down the ward between his tall house surgeon and Doctor Redfern, I couldn't help thinking he looked like a prisoner under police escort.'

The relief was magical. Ilse threw her head back and laughed out loud.

'Believe me, the pace would have been smarter if they really had got him on a charge! Oh, this is priceless! Red will love it.'

Sheila said in alarm: 'No, *please!* You mustn't tell him. I've dropped too many clangers already, and he wouldn't find it at all funny.'

Her fright was so real, Ilse Devon seemed in some extraordinary way reassured. She gave the girl a thoughtful look and said: 'You really believe that, don't you? You think he's quite inhuman. Oh, believe me, you're wrong. Timothy Redfern is a rather wonderful person.' She was half smiling now, and her eyes and voice were those of the woman who had driven off with him last night in the rain. 'In fact . . .'

Sheila never knew what she had been going to say, for Red himself was suddenly there in the doorway. Ilse looked startled. Sheila decided her surprise was quite genuine. Yet the way he had walked in suggested it was quite a habit to drop in at this time of day for a cup of tea and a chat. Ilse indeed drew forward a cup and saucer and lifted the teapot.

'Not for me, thanks. I just wanted a word with you about a case.'

Sheila jumped up, but he motioned to her not to go. Ilse seemed really put out. She doesn't like a threesome, Sheila thought, when one of the three is Red!

'Is it Stephen? I know you've been so worried about him all day.'

'No. A child with asthma. I've had Craikie on the phone to me.' He turned to Sheila. 'One of the G.P.s,' he said, bringing her into it before she could do a bolt as she had done from Dr Gannet's room that morning. 'Evangeline Hobbs had an alarming attack in the night and nearly frightened her parents to death. I'm admitting her tomorrow morning for a thorough investigation.'

Ilse cried out: 'But we'll get nowhere! When you had her in last February she fretted the whole time. The nurses were driven scatty.'

Red said dryly: 'This time I'm admitting Mrs Hobbs, too.'

'Seriously?'

'Of course. She'll come in every day while Evangeline is with us.' He turned to Sheila. 'This is a case where you and Mrs Devon can work together.'

Sheila was aware that Ilse stiffened, that her laugh was brittle as glass. 'I suppose you mean Miss Thorne is to put up with that awful woman's nagging and wind knitting wool for her while I give the child breathing exercises.'

'Nothing so simple. That child is spoilt and bored. I want to find what triggers off an attack. She may need help from you both in different ways. This time I'm hoping we shall get results. We'll go into all that tomorrow.' He glanced at his watch. 'I must be on my way, Dee has arranged for me to see a case of his at Scadcroft.'

'At this hour? And after such a day? How brutal!'

'He's had second thoughts about treatment,' was Red's only comment. 'I thought, if you're ready to leave——'

'But I'm not! I've just been telling Miss Thorne, Mr Dee has sent my day haywire. I'd like to put him on a charge.' Sheila looked up in alarm and found her smiling in a curious way. She glanced at the window and said: 'It's still raining. Would you be awfully sweet and run Miss Thorne home? I don't suppose it would take you much out of your way.'

Sheila started to protest. Red looked extremely put

out, and that made Sheila feel worse than ever. Was
that exactly what Ilse Devon intended? She was smiling
in such a friendly way, insisting, on Red's behalf, that
it would really be no trouble. Sheila would have thought
her thoughtful and kind, if it weren't for the poisonous
ideas Nurse Porson had planted. Suppose she wasn't
being kind at all, but deep, in some subtle way that left
one guessing? Putting Red in a position where he had
to give her a lift home, however inconvenient; testing
his loyalty and her power over him?

Yesterday it would have been quite a triumph to drive
home beside him. Tonight it was a humiliation.

She gave him directions and sat silent while he negotiated the city traffic. When she timidly ventured to
speak, it was to ask about Stephen. He gave her no
medical details. That was the sort of thing he discussed
with Mrs Devon. As if to point the difference between
them, he said that when Stephen's jet plane was airborne
it would be a good idea to start him shipbuilding.

' Bear it in mind, anyway. He won't be up to much
for a few days. He's really been through it. I was
anxious for Dee to have a look at that leg, and there
seemed to be one hold-up after another.'

Including a teddy-bear with a bandaged head, ought
Sheila, her face burning. She was thankful they had
reached the quiet avenue where she lived and the subject
couldn't be gone into further. She was out of the car
almost before it had stopped.

She stood in the rain, slim and small, bright drops
glistening in her hair, and thanked him for the lift. ' I
hope I haven't brought you out of your way.'

' Scadcroft happens to be in the opposite direction.'

She stammered an apology. If only she'd known . . .
But it was really Ilse's doing, and they were both uncomfortably aware of the fact. Suddenly he grinned.

' Well worth it if you can sneak model shipbuilding
into your syllabus. Whether or not it's laid down in the
Act!'

Mary Thorne had hurried to the door of the neat, well-painted semi. She watched the car disappear. 'Who was that, dear?' she enquired.

'Oh, one of the doctors.' Sheila's voice was muffled in the coat closet.

'Someone pretty high up. He has a lovely car,' said her father, appearing in the sitting-room doorway. 'And the garden so untidy since I had to go easy on the bending!'

'He didn't notice. He was in a hurry to be somewhere else.'

Her cheeks were very flushed. Now that it was too late, now that he had gone, she thought what a thrilling thing it had been to drive home with him through a pearl-grey spring dusk; and she found herself wishing with a sudden and frightening intensity that he had done it of his own free will, not at Ilse Devon's bidding.

After their meal, her parents went next door, as they often did, to watch television.

'You'll have homework to mark and lessons to prepare, or we'd coax you to come with us, Sheila dear.'

'I'm going to fit new guitar strings and work out my chords for some little songs,' she told them.

'The music-making won't disturb those who're really ill?' her mother asked doubtfully.

'They're soundproof. In the main ward the radio is on full blast most of the day!'

'Then however are the children to hear your guitar?'

'Oh, really! It's quite simple. We shall make our music out on the sun balcony. And to tell you the truth it's just to please a small boy called Gino Cort.'

'Cort?' said James Thorne, pausing in the doorway. 'Cort? I've heard that name somewhere. And quite recently.'

Sheila said lightly: 'You probably heard me saying it in my sleep. That child is so much on my mind.'

The foolish, wild thought came to her: As long as they don't hear me dreaming another name aloud. . . . *Red*

... *Red darling.* She tried it out, half mockingly, and for some absurd reason her eyes pricked with tears. *Red darling.* ... It sounded wonderful, but it wasn't a bit of use. *Kindly move over. You keep treading on my thoughts. Thank you, Doctor!* ... *Darling Red. Oh, I don't know whether I love you or hate you!* But one thing she did know. Since they met she hadn't had any peace of mind at all.

CHAPTER IV

'Well now, Mrs Hobbs,' said Sister Bain briskly, when she had a breather at last and could get round to Dr Redfern's new admission, 'my student nurses will be starting on the mid-morning drinks and I wonder if you'd like to help them while Miss Thorne has a little talk with Evangeline. Yes, I think that would be a good idea.'

Sheila thought so, too. At least Red had shown enough confidence in her to suggest she and Mrs Devon should work together on this case, and she was determined to show him that she had the training and the experience to sort out a young child's problems. He wasn't expecting her to get anywhere with Gino Cort; but if she succeeded with Evangeline ... And she *would* succeed. She would put everything else aside, if need be, because she simply had got to prove to him—and to Ilse Devon, too—that she wasn't just a spanner the Chief had chucked in the works, which was how they both made her feel!

She left her Spanish guitar with the new nylon strings and the scarlet shoulder ribbon in Sister's office, and the songs she had intended teaching her class out there on the balcony echoed in her mind like the cuckoo's wandering voice, while she set about the business of making friends with Evangeline.

She was a wheezy, thin child of four, small for her age, with a bouncing, talkative mother who wore a very tight skirt and jumper and, like the spring, was busting out all over. She looked down her nose when Sister suggested helping the nurses and said that wasn't what she was here for, she had to look after Evangeline.

Sister made no comment, but the look she gave Sheila said more plainly than words: If you can take it from there, good luck to you!

Mrs Hobbs sat knitting furiously away at another tight jumper and telling Sheila her tale of woe, breaking off every now and then to speak sharply to the child. The comical thing was, Evangeline was playing around, perfectly content as long as she had her mother in sight, and it was hard to believe she had driven the ward scatty when she was admitted in February, and nearly frightened her parents to death with the last attack of asthma.

'Come here, Evangeline, the lady wants to talk to you. Put that toy down, you don't know what germs there might be on it.'

'If the children were infectious, they'd be isolated,' Sheila pointed out.

'Well, we can't be too careful. She's so delicate. Evangeline! Don't wipe your hands down the front of your dress! . . . Yes, she's been delicate from the start. I was in labour forty-eight hours with her.'

'Shall we sit at this little table and do a puzzle?' said Sheila quickly, holding out her hand to the child.

But Mrs Hobbs moved her chair up to the little table and gave the full history of what she had been through in order to bring Evangeline into the world.

'And of course we're so tied. Every time we plan to go out of an evening, she has an attack. My next-door neighbour has offered many a time to baby-sit, but it never comes off. You'd almost think Evangeline *knew*, though we never say a word in front of her about going out.'

But a duller child than Evangeline would guess there was something afoot, thought Sheila.

'Mind you, she's very precious. We had an awful time with her as a baby. Nothing suited her. We must have tried a dozen baby foods. Evangeline, if you wipe your dirty hands on your dress again I'll give you a slap. Don't they make some work? Everything she has is hand-sewn, and the smocking on that little dress wasn't done in a minute, I can tell you! Evangeline, you heard me! What's a handkerchief for?'

'They're just brewing up in the ward kitchen,' Sheila said hastily. 'I'm sure you'd like a cup of tea. It's just through the swing-doors.'

'No, dear, I mustn't leave Evangeline. It's that red-haired doctor with the deep voice she's scared of. If he so much as touched her she'd scream the place down. . . . Shocking how they keep you waiting at this place. And then they don't really tell you anything.'

When a nurse popped up to say the doctor would see Mrs Hobbs now, Sheila didn't notice Evangeline showing any signs of terror. She was looking longingly at the small dolls and the bright bits of lace and satin spread out on the table in front of some lucky small girls. Sheila risked keeping the Boss Man waiting a minute.

'When you come back to the ward, Evangeline, you shall choose a little doll for your own—and she's going to have very smart clothes indeed.'

But she couldn't really expect it to be as easy as that! There were all sorts of tests and investigations to be made, no doubt. Evangeline didn't come back. And meanwhile Sheila couldn't stand twiddling her thumbs. The interruptions were so disheartening, she never could spend long enough with one child. But at least she was getting to know them, winning their confidence. Their faces lit up when she came round from bed to bed to mark their lessons. Red, who had hated school, might find that hard to believe! But even he must surely see that the children gave less trouble, now they were kept busy; and that she was able to provide the thing they missed most: work and play shared with other children.

She gathered a few of the up-and-about ones round the bed of a child who couldn't get up at all, and even if they were only reading aloud or answering some little countryside quiz, they felt it was a party! So many little boys wanted to help Stephen with his model plane, she had to hide it away in his locker till he could tackle it himself. Meanwhile, among some tatty old comics which had gone the rounds till they fell to pieces, she had found him a book to read and he was eager to tell her all about it.

'Swot?' said the Registrar's voice, heavy with disapproval. He had suddenly loomed up at the foot of the bed. 'Now look here, the boy isn't up to it yet. This school idea can be carried too far!'

Sheila silently passed him the book.

'Um. *Yarns of the Merchant Navy.* Well, that's different.'

Sheila gave him an indignant look. Didn't he credit her with any sense at all? 'I suppose I should have submitted the book for your approval first, Doctor.'

His smile, friendly and rueful, took her utterly by surprise.

'I apologize. I couldn't have made a better choice myself. When I was Stephen's age I gave my knee a bash on the vaulting horse at school. I hadn't anything as spectacular as this to show for it.' He waved a hand at the complicated traction system. 'But I don't think I ever felt so sorry for myself, before or since. You see, my uncle, a retired sea captain, had just bought a sailing dinghy and he was to have taken me with him for the trials. It was what I wanted to do most in the world, and the weather was perfect—I could hear the wind in the trees and see the clouds racing across a blue sky outside my bedroom window. And there I was, a useless hulk laid up on the hard!'

Stephen said urgently: 'But you did sail in her later. Tell Miss Thorne about the smashing adventure you had off the Mumbles. Oh, *please*, sir!'

'Smashing is the right word. We were tacking off a lee shore, when——' Suddenly he looked embarrassed and finished awkwardly: 'It wouldn't have the slightest interest for Miss Thorne.'

'It would, too!' Sheila's eyes were shining. 'I know that Welsh coast, and——'

'Excuse me.' Ilse Devon's voice cut in, annoyed and flustered. She had come hurrying across the ward, and now she said vexedly: 'I'm having trouble with Evangeline Hobbs. I knew it was too good to be true, the way she was behaving. Mrs Hobbs brought her down to the department, as you instructed, with a note about the rhythmical breathing and the relaxation exercises. But as soon as she got inside the door and saw where she was, she began making the most awful to-do, crying and holding her breath. She gave us quite a fright. And all because she'd been promised a doll when she came back to the ward!'

Sheila said in distress: 'I did promise her a doll—and she went off so happily. Mrs Hobbs told me she was scared of——' She bit that off, not daring to look in Red's direction.

Mrs Devon gave a brittle laugh. 'So that's it! We don't bribe the children here.' Perhaps she was remembering Sister's famous jar of barley sugar as she added: 'At least we don't promise something fantastic like a beautiful new doll and have to disappoint the child, after all.'

'It's nothing like that. They're just little clothes-peg dolls on which I've painted faces and hair.' How ridiculous that sounded! 'The children dress them in scraps from my mother's work-bag. I put one aside for Evangeline because I saw she had taken a fancy to it and I thought it would help her over the bad moment when she had to see the doctor.'

Ilse's eyebrows went up. She looked scandalized. Giving Red an amused side-glance, she asked: 'Do you make him out such an ogre when you tell the children fairy stories?'

In a small, hurried voice Sheila offered to fetch the doll. Or should she pop down herself with it, so that Evangeline would see she hadn't forgotten her promise?

'By all means.' There was something in his voice. Was he amused or offended? 'Let's have peace and quiet restored, down below. The child is to have a sleep after these exercises, and this afternoon you might see how she gets on with the other children—if you can coax her away from her mother.'

'I brought along my guitar. We'll be having music and it should be fun.'

'Splendid. I'll be interested to know if that helps her. The child is coiled up tight like a spring.' He glanced at Ilse, who nodded agreement. Red said thoughtfully: 'There's such a thing as too much loving—or should we say unwise loving? This child isn't mothered but smothered!'

Sheila found courage to say: 'That isn't Gino's problem, is it? But he's a bundle of nerves, too!'

Red's eyes were blue and piercing as he looked at her.

'The Browns did all they could—and with no hope of gain. It's just unlucky the child is a misfit.'

Ilse said: 'What can you expect, with such a father? He hasn't once tried to see the child or asked after him in eight years!'

It was all true, but a piece of the puzzle was missing. Sheila had seen the child terribly distressed for Stephen's sake. He wasn't cold and stupid, as they thought. And how could they be so sure the father was a feckless no-good? He might have done what he thought best for the child by leaving him with the Browns. Would anyone ever know the whole truth?

The children loved her guitar with the scarlet ribbon, and they sang like a cage of nightingales to the softly strummed chords. But there was nothing in it for Gino! He lay quite still, hunched under the bedclothes. He might have been tone-deaf or fast asleep for all the response Sheila got from him.

'And I'd hoped so much from it,' she confessed to Ilse, who paused in the short corridor between the two sets of swing doors for a chat as Sheila was putting her things away after school.

'Never mind, I'm sure the others had fun.'

'Oh, they did. Evangeline began dancing to the music. Then her hair-ribbon came off and Mrs Hobbs hurried her away to be tidied up, so we had a scene.'

'That woman!' Ilse looked dangerous. 'She was very rude to Doctor Redfern, and after all his trouble she insists on taking the child home.'

'Oh, *no*! I had such plans for tomorrow.'

'Tomorrow,' said Ilse, 'has a way of coming unstuck.' She said it with a world of bitterness, that haunted look in her eyes again.

'I thought we might start a percussion band—triangles and bells and drums. And a few of the older children have played recorders at school.' Seeing Ilse's face, she added hastily: 'If Doctor Gannet approves.'

'You'll soon know. He'll be back next week. He's a pet, but just not *with* it. Goodness knows what new ideas he'll bring back from that congress! Mrs Gannet is the sweetest person. They've both been awfully good to me, you know.' As Ilse spoke, her face went soft. Then she said hastily: 'Look who's here. You won't mind if I make myself scarce?'

It was Mrs Hobbs who had come back for Evangeline's little doll. Sheila found it for her.

'I'm sorry you're taking her home, Mrs Hobbs. I think we could have helped her.'

'I've wasted enough time here,' snapped Mrs Hobbs. 'Do you know what that doctor had the cheek to say when I asked if there wasn't some new treatment? He said the best thing I could do was to have another baby. What do you think of that? And coming from him, a bachelor! Though one of the nurses was telling me over our cup of tea——'

Nurse Porson gossiping again, thought Sheila disgustedly. She got rid of Mrs Hobbs quickly. Red had given her such good advice, really. But a new baby to keep her busy, and Evangeline given a chance to stand on her own feet. . . . Or was the damage done already? Would the attacks be more frequent and alarming still when the mother's attention was divided?

'What you need,' said Dick Sawley, looming up in front of her, 'is to throw off this load of care and have a ball. In other words, how about Saturday night? Just supposing I'm lucky enough to get a couple of hours off. A houseman is——'

'I know. A dogsbody. But surely you get time off? Or is the weekend a luxury for Registrars?'

'Red is a seven-days-a-week man,' said Dick promptly and with pride.

'Then it's a good thing he hasn't a wife, she'd never stand for it,' said Sheila, without stopping to think.

He looked at her sideways. 'I daresay his devotion to duty doesn't go down too well in certain quarters!'

There it was again! Everyone hinted that these two were more than friends; that they had some bond which had brought him here to be near her, and which gave Ilse the right to say in that special tone of voice: *Red darling, what a wonderful surprise!*

Sheila said a little stridently: 'But he shouldn't expect you to work seven days a week, too!'

Dick laughed and pulled a face. 'I'm going to wangle time off to take you on the town. That's a promise.'

Sheila suddenly felt uneasy. She didn't want Dick Sawley getting ideas! She hastily explained that her parents might have fixed something and she liked to fit in with their plans. She'd have lessons to prepare, anyway.

'Don't give me that!' said Dick disgustedly. 'You're as bad as old Red!'

'Well, there it is. Perhaps some other time. And thanks all the same, Dick.'

To certain people she was an intruder on the ward, but Dick had gone out of his way to smooth out the snags and she was grateful. Already, in spite of setbacks, this job gripped her as no other could, and she was determined to prove herself equal to it.

Perhaps Miss Furlong, the retired headmistress who had come in hitherto once or twice a week to read aloud, felt the same way about it. She turned up that Friday afternoon with a neat parcel under one arm and waylaid Sheila as she emerged from the store-room.

'The ward teacher, I believe.'

Have I got chalk on my nose, thought Sheila, or is there an aura?

'Here. These may be of use. Books.' Miss Furlong thrust the parcel into her hands. 'The whole set-up is changed, of course. High time it was put on a proper footing. Disgraceful procrastination and cheese-paring by the authority. I wish you luck.'

'How kind,' said Sheila, unwrapping the parcel. 'Fairy stories!'

'Perhaps you disapprove of fairy stories? They're out of fashion. Realism. That's what they insist on nowadays.'

'My children love fairy stories,' Sheila said firmly. 'We have a little girl called Popsy——' She hesitated, plunged. 'Please don't think I'm taking advantage of your kindness, but if ever you can spare an hour——'

'My dear,' said Miss Furlong, her face a sunrise, 'if you knew how hard it's been to stay away! I did think of offering an afternoon at the convalescent place, but it's very far out and the bus service is terrible. You're sure I won't be in the way?'

'Indeed, you're a godsend! There are hectic moments when I feel like the old woman in the shoe!'

'Lead on, Macduff!' said Miss Furlong, joyously striding into the ward.

After school, as they walked down the corridor together, Miss Furlong said earnestly: 'Just send an S O S any time and I'll be here like a shot. Holidays. Emergencies. Count on me.'

'I will,' said Sheila gratefully, though she felt sure this wasn't laid down in the Act!

Round a corner came Matron, stately in dark green with her tiny muslin cap; the chairman of the committee strode beside her, and Mr Porson and Mr Mercks panted in the rear. Sheila and Miss Furlong stood aside to let them pass. At the last moment Mr Porson glanced in their direction, saw Miss Furlong and went beetroot red.

'Good afternoon, Mr Porson,' she said in a deep, significant tone.

Mr Porson gave her a baleful look and was almost running as he disappeared from sight.

'Not a bit of good,' said Miss Furlong, shaking her head. 'He can't escape!'

'From what?' asked Sheila, startled and amused.

'From the grace of God,' said Miss Furlong. 'Perhaps you don't know Joe Porson? Really he's a very unpleasant, spiteful little man. One afternoon I was here reading to the children, the committee had been round to look at the new decorations and he was holding forth—he insisted there had been some corruption and palm-greasing in the tenders for the work. His language was disgraceful. I followed him out and told him so. And I informed him that when I reached home I should pray for him.'

Humour glinted in her eye.

'To an aggressive, self-confident little man like Joe Porson there's nothing so infuriating as being prayed for. Every time we meet I give him a certain look, and he knows I shall hurry home and get straight down on my knees.' Head tilted, she considered for a moment. 'There must be *some* good in him. He gives many hours of service on the hospital committee and one hears he's putting up for the City Council. Now I ask you, can this be love of power alone? No, of course not.' She smiled triumphantly. 'And one of these days the grace of God is going to grab him when he isn't looking.'

Sheila had the uneasy feeling it wouldn't happen soon enough. Mr Porson would make trouble yet!

Miss Furlong said confidentially: 'I advise you to try the same tactics, my dear, if that bully of a Registrar makes things difficult.' She gave Sheila a little dig with her elbow. 'You know who I mean. Captain Bligh. The Red Admiral.'

It was wildly funny. Sheila felt a compulsion to add Long John Silver and Captain Diggory Piper to the list.

She said firmly: 'There's no need for tactics, I assure you! Doctor Redfern and I keep out of one another's way, it's as simple as that. And once I leave the hospital I don't give the man another thought.'

Perhaps she made it just a little too emphatic, or perhaps the flushed cheek and kindled eye betrayed her; for Miss Furlong was looking at her in a peculiar way, almost reproachfully. If the woman dares to go home and pray for me . . . she thought hotly, suddenly knowing just how Joe Porson felt. The next minute that seemed absurd. Miss Furlong was priceless—and so well-meaning. It was ridiculous to get into a state just because Timothy Redfern's name was dragged in! What she needed, of course, was a gay, busy weekend with the hospital put resolutely out of mind.

As it happened, her parents had planned nothing except a little gardening and the weekend felt long and empty. Many and many a time she found herself thinking of the Children's Ward, wondering what emergency had come in to keep them all with their noses to the grindstone; whether Dick had found a pretty nurse to keep him company on Saturday night, and why Red drove himself and his team so relentlessly. They did snatch some off-duty, but for him there seemed to be no let-up at all.

Not even on a Monday morning. The Chief was expected back, there was an Outpatient clinic and Sister Bain was having a blitz on the ward. She had clean sheets on all the beds and the children tucked up safely, however 'dancy and prancy' their legs might feel. Sheila rushed round with tracing books and cut-outs to keep them good. Then she had to organize things on the balcony. It was halfway through the morning before she found a spare minute to help Stephen put the finishing touches to his model plane. She wound up the elastic motor, yards and yards of it, ready for the maiden flight.

There was a hush over the ward. They were all, she imagined, waiting for the take-off.

'Here goes,' said Stephen. 'Oh boy, oh boy, how's that for a flyer?'

The little plane was airborne, the children cheered. Too late Sheila, who had been so engrossed in winding that propellor, saw Dr Gannet's procession just entering the ward. She gave a gasp of dismay, and all the children seemed to echo it in a long, falling sigh. The plane made a curve in the air and crashed at Dr Gannet's feet, just wreckage. She knew a moment of sick regret for Stephen's sake. All those hours of work! That was swamped by Red's frown, Sister Bain's look of outrage. Dr Gannet picked up the plane and trotted across, and of course the procession had to tag after him.

He was beaming. 'Splendid, splendid! This is just what I hoped. I want to see the children busy with their work and play, not shut off in a world apart.' He was making a whirlwind round, and somehow Sheila found herself swept along with him. He would address a remark to her, turn his head to include the Registrar, point a finger at Ilse Devon or Sister Bain, as they hurried to keep up with him. 'Surely some of these children ought to be up and about, Sister? And I'd like to see more beds pushed out on the balcony. It may not be Swiss mountain air, but we don't want to treat them like hothouse plants, surely!'

He halted by Norina's bed and admired her painting.

'Splendid, splendid!' He stared hard at *I love Elvis* with its flowery border and asked Red in an undertone: 'What does it mean?'

'Much the same as *I Dig Adam*, sir,' said the Registrar gravely.

'Aha! Of course Adam goes with digging and delving, but . . .' He looked completely baffled, then brightened up as a new idea struck him. 'Indoor gardening. That's something we might have a go at, don't you think, Miss Thorne?' He beamed round at them in a fatherly way. 'All sorts of things occurred to me on the journey and I made jottings. We must have a get-together. Oh, not in the firm's time!' He chuckled. 'You must come to us for coffee and sandwiches one evening. Would Saturday suit you, Miss Thorne? And how about you two?' He looked towards Ilse and Red; then, suddenly doubtful: 'Though I do seem to remember Mrs Gannet and I have some engagement.'

Sheila fervently hoped they had. It was one matter to discuss her scheme of work with the Chief—she had been impatient for that chance—but a social occasion at his home, where she'd be agonizingly aware that she was playing gooseberry to Ilse and Red, that was something she couldn't face.

They had reached Popsy's bed, and suddenly it was a serious medical consultation. Sheila slipped away. She had to comfort Stephen for the disaster to his aeroplane. But it wasn't comfort the boy needed, it was a few strips of balsa wood and a new tube of cement so that he could repair the plane before his parents came to see him tomorrow.

'My dad would fly her for me. That'd be super!'

A tightness came into Sheila's throat. The Chief was right, they weren't hothouse plants, they were tough. They had all the grit in the world.

'As a matter of fact,' she told Stephen, 'I'm going shopping after lunch. Tell me exactly what I must ask for.'

When she saw Gino she knew he was worrying about the crashed plane, as he'd worried secretly about Stephen's leg being 'cut down'. She smiled down at him.

'Do you know, Stephen says he can easily mend that wing. His father will help him to fly the plane and you must be there to watch. I'll tell Sister.'

Gino gave her a fierce look. 'Don't you tell Sister nothing. I'll shut my eyes, then I won't see it crash.'

But all dreams don't crash, she wanted to tell him. If only he could look forward to tomorrow, as the others did! If only he wanted something, asked for something. . . .

She cut short her lunch to go hunting for a toyshop. The hospital was in the old quarter of the city, and she was still hunting round when a drenching, sleety rain came on. She sheltered on the steps of a shabby theatre before making a dash to the toyshop she had spotted at the opposite corner. There was a small queue at the box office, and a charwoman in stout boots and a man's cap worn back to front was sloshing muddy water over the foyer. Once, Sheila didn't doubt, this had been a fashionable place, though now sadly fallen from gentility. The marble floor was still handsome and there were two potted palms and a lavish splash of colour on the billboards. It was something to see a theatre still attracting custom at the box office in these days.

'The Fun and Laughter Show' was what the banner promised. Well, that was fine, too. Just the weather for it, and good luck to you, mates! thought Sheila, glancing at the posters.

A pair of eyes leapt out at her. A narrow, handsome, sulky face. A lot of dark hair. Gino's eyes and face and hair. The likeness was so uncanny, it turned her heart over. She read the lettering splashed right across the bill:

The Television Sensation: Victor Cort and his Swinging Fiddle.

CHAPTER V

Sheila stared and stared.

'If you want to join the queue, dearie, don't mind me,' said the cleaning lady, shifting her bucket.

As Sheila still stood there with wide, startled eyes, she said encouragingly: 'Folks want cheering up these days, don't they, love? It's a good show, though I can't say I'm carried away by the comedian. Between you and me, dearie, his jokes haven't just got whiskers on them, they've grown beards. The trick cyclists are smart, I must say, and the band gives you plenty of noise for your money. But what's pulling them in is this here chap with the fiddle.'

She wiped her hands, surveyed the wet floor critically and stood beside Sheila, breathing hard.

'Ten minutes on telly—and they're stars!' she remarked profoundly. 'Mind you, this Victor Cort ain't just a space man, here today and gone tomorrow, like the kids with guitars. He can play. When he's swinging it with the band he has all the heads nodding and the feet tapping—they'd be twisting in the aisles if the usherettes didn't keep a sharp look-out. Oh, yes, he sends them, all right! And then he comes up front with the spotlight on him, and the band fades out, and he goes into his gipsy music, soft as a kettle starting to sing. But before you know where you are, that fiddle of his is laughing and sobbing. And you're remembering the first time you were in love, and it's like you've been going around all this time with a broken heart and you never knew it till now, and there's tears running down your face.'

She gave the man on the poster a special sort of smile: a lumpy little woman with a tough job and an ailing husband, for whom Victor Cort's violin could unlock the door to forgotten worlds of romance.

'Then the lights go up, see, and they're clapping like

crazy and wiping their eyes. Yes, dearie, folks want cheering up these days. But they can clap and call out till the interval's over, he never takes a curtain call. Temperamental, dearie. That shows he's a *real* musician, don't it?'

Having disposed of the queue, the box office girl poked her head out of there and said in a nasal sing-song: 'Seats in all parts tonight. But if it's for Saturday, I may as well tell you straight off I've only got singles left except for two seats on the back row of the fauteuils.'

She pronounced it 'tuttles' and when she pointed to the plan Sheila saw she meant the front stalls.

She was tapping on the glass with her pencil, impatient to nip out for a cup of hot coffee while the cleaner was still there to give her a signal if any customers came along and before the manager got back from his lunch.

'Do you want them or don't you?'

Without meaning to at all, Sheila heard herself say: 'I'll take them.' She was fumbling in her purse, and then she was out in the street in such a daze that she didn't even notice it had come on to rain harder than ever, and was almost at the hospital before she remembered Stephen's balsa wood and had to trudge all the way back for it.

Her thoughts were whirling like fallen leaves driven by the wind. Queer, disquieting thoughts they were, too. Victor Cort was here, in this town, and he had made no attempt to see that child. But of course he couldn't know that Gino was ill in hospital—nor even that the Browns had left Edgware. But he should have known. Even if there was no place for a child in a wandering musician's life, he could have kept in touch. It was a shocking and wicked thing to go off and leave him utterly to strangers, without even bothering about legal safeguards.

She knew that without his written consent the child couldn't be adopted. Or could the court make an order after a certain length of time had elapsed with no trace of the parents? She understood why the hospital people saw Victor Cort as the villain of the piece. But every time she felt like agreeing with them and feeling sorry for the Browns, she remembered Gino as he was now: a lonely, mixed-up, suspicious little boy. Somehow the Browns had failed him. She had been wishing with all her heart that father and child could be brought together —now she wasn't sure that would really solve anything.

She was bursting to tell someone her news—but who? She could guess how Sister Bain would take it. Red would tell her to mind her own business, which was to give the children lessons, not pry into their family affairs. And the Chief, though he was so keen on treating the child 'all in one piece', home background and health and everything taken together, was in the thick of things after his absence abroad and it was hardly the moment to go worrying him. Even if she dared!

That was settled for her. She was sitting beside Popsy, telling her a story and holding the book so that the child could see the pictures as she talked, when quite suddenly Dr Gannet appeared at the bedside. He liked to pop in without the ceremony of his big round and give them a surprise. If he knew what a state that threw Sister into! Just now he'd caught her at her lunch-tray. 'Don't mind me, Sister. And for goodness' sake, my dear girl, don't scald your mouth with hot coffee on my account!' But of course she had to gulp it down and get on the phone to send an urgent call round for the Registrar, while Dick Sawley got the results of Popsy's tests lined up.

After all this frantic activity they found the Chief perched on the edge of Popsy's bed and earnestly discussing with the ward teacher special equipment she ought to put in for. He had a passion for gadgets and dug a catalogue out of his pocket. Book-rests and bed-tables, apparatus to throw on the ceiling or a slanted screen whole pages of print and illustrations, for use with children who were being nursed flat on their backs.

When Red loomed up, with Sister panting behind him, Dr Gannet greeted them both with a beaming smile.

'We're going to put in for an epidiascope. They have pictures on the ceiling at the orthopaedic hospitals. Why shouldn't our children?'

'Why indeed, sir,' said Red in a correct tone, keeping his thoughts to himself. All this and indoor gardening, too! He coughed. 'Mr Bracewell is on his way, sir.'

Mr Bracewell was the heart surgeon, and Sheila needed no stronger hint to make herself scarce. She slipped away, leaving them to their mysteries. 'Cardiac catheterization under X-ray.' 'Definite fixed splitting.' It was double-dutch to her, as it was to the children. But as she went about her work she was intensely aware that a matter of life and death was being decided behind the screens.

Nurse Porson, pop-eyed and in a starchy flutter, came looking for her.

'Drop everything. They want you,' she said quickly.

'Me?'

'That's right. How do you do it? The kiddie keeps asking for you, and I suppose they have to humour her.'

They hurried down the ward together. Red stepped from behind the screens. Things were going wrong with an important consultation and the strain showed.

'Look, the surgeon needs to see this child in a relaxed state, not under stress; but we can't seem able to make her understand this isn't another big test. He merely wants to listen to her "murmur", look at the reports and get on friendly terms before she's moved to the cardiac unit.'

Then Dr Gannet popped out and had his little say.

'The child is apprehensive, Miss Thorne. Naturally they don't like the tests—taking the barium drink and sitting in the darkened X-ray room while the heart's action is screened. But we already have the radiologist's report on all that.'

And Sister, hovering, upset at the way things were

going: 'She's always been so *good*. Now if it were Gino——'

Sheila met the child's anxious, pleading look and forgot everything else. She came close, held Popsy's hand and smiled down at her.

'Such a fuss for nothing! Popsy, how could you? There isn't any funny white pudding today. You don't even have to sit in the Punch-and-Judy box! The doctor just wants to say hello.'

And what Popsy wanted, after all that, was simply to hear the end of the interrupted story! It was such an anticlimax, Sheila really didn't know where to look, for embarrassment. She promised hastily that she would finish the story and show her the pictures again as soon as Sister said it was convenient. That did the trick. Popsy relaxed, and even smiled shyly at the doctors.

But Red was frowning. Sheila was sure the whole incident annoyed him excessively. As she received the Chief's kindly nod of thanks and dismissal she could see the Registrar frowning away behind him. And half an hour later, on the balcony, he was telling her why. In the cardiac ward visiting was kept down to the minimum. The parents were allowed in for a few minutes once a day—suitably gowned and masked—and no other visitors at all.

Sheila felt sick with dismay. She had put her foot in it again.

'Most of these cases are very ill, and with damaged hearts there's a severe risk of infection. Not to mention the fact that before the operation the parents might frighten a child through their own anxiety and tension. Popsy's mother will keep in touch by phone, of course.'

Sheila's mouth suddenly felt dry.

'Mr Bracewell has decided to operate?'

'Tomorrow.'

'And it's . . . risky?'

'Any heart operation is tricky, and in these A.S.D. cases the success depends on the size of hole—which the surgeon won't know till he opens it up, though our pressure readings will have given him a good idea.' He frowned thoughtfully. 'It's been a doubtful case. The child was fairly well till recently. Then their own doctor saw a change and sent her to the Outpatient clinic. She seemed to me a very ill child, so I got her in for observation, hoping Bracewell would soon have a bed vacant and slip her on to his list. She's been lucky.'

'Lucky!' whispered Sheila.

'She might have had months to wait. I admit myself at fault for not making all this clear to the mother.'

Which was as near as the Boss Man would ever get to an apology, thought Sheila, a smile glimmering. Then her eyes went dark with distress again.

'I shouldn't have promised her that story. She'll be expecting me. I feel terrible about it.'

'Actually Bracewell is going to stretch a point and let you have five minutes with her as soon as she's settled in. He thinks it will give her a better night.' And then he said one of those utterly unexpected sweet things. 'I think so, too. The way you've won the confidence of these children——'

Sheila swallowed hard. 'I'll be so scared.'

'Rubbish. You face your lions like a very Daniel.' His smile held so much understanding, so much kindness, she forgot on the instant every harsh thing she'd thought about him. 'It can't have been easy finding your feet at M.G.H., but you've gone a long way already.'

She said with frankness: 'I'm afraid of what I'll see across there.'

'You'll see new-born babies and children up to sixteen, and the few adult cases, who are nursed in private cubicles, by the way. Those kids may be short of breath because of their heart trouble, but they make up for it in high spirits. Discuss their operations like real old-timers—and that means the new ones know what to expect and find it less terrifying. Some of the hole-in-the-heart children who've lived with their disability look forward eagerly to being "made new".' His mouth went down. ' Little do they know what anxiety we and their parents go through!'

She nodded slowly. ' And when will Popsy . . . when must we start keeping our fingers crossed for her?'

' Start now. In the morning I'll be preparing her for transfusion. We use a big vein in the ankle—under a local anaesthetic, of course. They feel very little, but it's messy and fiddly.' He spoke patiently, as if he realized now how important a simple, clear explanation might be for someone concerned about the child. ' The nurse will distract her by talking or reading her a story while I do the cut-down.' He gave her a keen look. ' Might be an idea to have *you* there.'

Sheila made a little wincing movement.

' No. It would be different if I didn't know the child.'

' Ah! Now perhaps you see what I'm driving at. You can help these children tremendously as long as you're not emotionally involved. That's where the parents are at a disadvantage. You see, they *love* the child.'

There was pain in Sheila's eyes. ' Some children need to be loved before I can help them.'

' You're asking to be hurt,' said Red. ' I'm warning you. Don't take to your heart a child who'll forget you —along with the rest of his hospital experience—as fast as he can, once he leaves here.'

He followed her glance as she cast a quick look towards the other end of the balcony. His lips tightened. ' I don't know if Sister has told you we're putting Gino's name down for convalescence out at Scadcroft. They have the dickens of a waiting list, but if I can get him there, at least it'll delay the decision about his future.'

Sheila's heart gave a jolt. This was her chance to impart the great news. But now that it came to the point, something held her back; perhaps the certainty of

Red's disapproval. She said hurriedly: 'I know the almoner thinks he may have to go to a Children's Home, but Mrs Brown might want him back, after all, mightn't she? Or his real father might turn up.'

'His real father!' It was spoken with angry contempt. 'How would you expect a mixed-up kid to cope with that situation? No, let's hope no ill wind blows the fellow here.'

Emotionally involved. He had used big words for such a simple thing. You couldn't work with these children without giving them something of your heart. It went deeper than lessons or nursing care or occupation for a bored moment. It was the vital thing.

Nurse Velta came up to her as she was going across to fit a happy ending to Popsy's fairy story.

'That Popsy is the bluest baby I ever done see. Oh, lordy, yes! Like she's been stuffing herself with blueberry pie. You give her my lucky parrot's feathers, Teacher ma'am, and she gonna come out pink like a nice little pig.'

Sheila turned the gaily coloured bunch of feathers between her fingers.

'No lucky charm will do that miracle, Velta! But I have faith in the surgeon's skill.'

'Sure! Mr Bracewell gonna do his best for Popsy, and my lucky feathers gonna put magic in his fingers, and we all gonna hope and pray. That's the way it is.'

That's the way it is. . . . Next morning at early Mass, Nurse Connell lit a candle for Popsy, and once or twice Sheila saw her lips move silently as she went about her tasks. The ward was tense. Sister Bain snapped at everybody, found dust in the unlikeliest places and complained of the state of the floor. When coffee break came round, she glanced at her watch and said: 'They'll be starting just about now.' She blew her nose hard. 'You go through it with every child. There are times when I feel I can't take it any more.' The phone rang. She jumped to it. As she put down the receiver she said sharply: 'That's Mrs Devon. Two children should have gone down for exercises in the bath. What's Staff thinking about this morning?' Off she went, war in her eye.

Waiting for news. . . . Sheila seemed to live through again the terrible anxiety of her father's illness. Her thoughts weren't on her work. They were with Popsy. She didn't think any of the children noticed, but as she went from bed to bed on the balcony, Gino plucked at her skirt. She had given him some drawing paper like the others and saw that for once he was trying to please her. He had covered the sheet with little matchstick men in action.

'Gino, what an exciting picture! Are they gardening?' she asked, before it suddenly came to her that what she had taken for a flower-bed was an operating table and the enormous sun over it a theatre lamp. Her throat felt constricted. 'Popsy?'

The little boy's enormous dark eyes, like brown velvet with a fringe of lashes, looked up at her.

'It was just a teeny weeny hole and they've mended it,' he said.

For a minute she couldn't speak. He had been aware of her distress and this was his way of trying to comfort her. She said in a croak: 'Yes, *of course*.' And prayed it was true.

Actually she was the first to hear the news. She was passing along the corridor during the afternoon when Dick Sawley came out of the cardiac unit, the doors swinging behind him. She halted, absolutely incapable of moving or speaking, and looked at him. But his face was so bright, he simply couldn't be on his way back with tragic tidings. Then he gave her the thumbs-up sign.

'She's all right. It was straightforward. I've just had a quick word with Bracewell's H.S. You know they're always thankful when they find no complication —such as a blockage which means they mustn't close it up. There are critical hours ahead, of course; but at this stage we can feel pretty sure of the outcome. The parents will be allowed to see her tonight.'

Sheila's face crumpled. 'I'm so thankful.' The relief was intense. She blinked away tears. 'Silly of me.' (And how scathing Red would be!) 'But you see, this is my *first*.'

Dick said promptly: 'Something to celebrate.' He put on a determined look. 'Here we go again. What are you doing on Saturday night?'

Sheila hesitated only a moment.

'As a matter of fact I have two tickets for the show at the variety theatre,' she told him.

'I expected you to tell me you were going to the Chief's place.'

'It's been put off. I told him I wasn't free.'

'You cried off—for my sake?' His candid features showed delight and unbelief. 'Sheila, you're a good sport.' Then he looked crestfallen. 'But what I had in mind wasn't a Dutch treat. Well. My share will be a real slap-up meal before the show. Okay?'

Sheila said hastily: 'We can fix all that later. Do hurry with the wonderful news about Popsy. Sister is on pins. They *all* are.'

'It won't be news by the time I get there. Theatre Sister will have phoned. They just feel they have to keep me out of mischief, chasing round with messages. . . . Didn't I tell you, I'm the muggins.'

But he went off in a great hurry, all the same.

And I must tell Gino, thought Sheila. Her eyes pricked again when she thought of his picture: such a crowd of little matchstick men jostling round the enormous operating table, and the lamp with rays like a sun. She thought: I'll treasure it always.

And once again her heart beat very fast when she thought of Saturday night. Dick Sawley, after all, would be the first of the Chief's team to see Victor Cort. Perhaps he would prove a good ally. At least she would get a man's estimate of Gino's father.

How would the evening turn out? Poor Dick, his
'real slap-up meal' wasn't the bit she looked forward
to! It was seeing that poster come to life, hearing
the music that could hold a whole theatre under its
spell. . . .

A houseman's weekend was chancy. She couldn't
bear it if something turned up at the last moment and he
wasn't free.

Then she thought: With or without Dick, I'm going to
see that show.

And she found herself wishing for Nurse Velta's little
bunch of magic feathers, because she had so strongly, so
insistently, the feeling that Gino's whole future depended
on Saturday evening.

CHAPTER VI

By the weekend Popsy was 'doing nicely' on the
progress list for phone enquiries and 'driving us up the
wall' according to the SOS Sheila got from the unit.
She found another couple of children there who were
well enough to feel restless and bored, and she had to
use her wits to set them lessons which would keep them
busy without getting over-tired. Their eyes lit up whenever she appeared, and the nurses were just as welcoming. In this place where she had seemed an intrusive
stranger, she already had as much work as one pair of
hands and an eager, hopeful spirit could cope with.

The difficult thing was still how to be in two places at
once—like that bird of Nurse Connell's! And on Friday
afternoon as she was hurrying across from the cardiac
unit she turned a corner and bumped into the Boss Man.
It was a hard collision and her books, papers and a box
of coloured pencils were all spilled on the floor.

'Steady there! The crazy way you rush round,' said
Red, holding her by the arms.

She was flushed and breathless and blurted an apology as she crouched down and began scrabbling for her papers. Red helped. And that brought him so close, she was looking straight into those very blue eyes. She stood up hastily.

'Look,' he said in a severe tone, 'it isn't a life and death matter, getting back to the ward. When you're tempted to flap, remember these kids got along all right before a ward teacher was even thought of.'

'I know,' said Sheila, and she couldn't help giving him a flying glance which held reproach. He made all her hard work seem of such little account.

'It isn't a ha'porth of use telling you to ease off when you're rushing round with some new project on your mind,' said Red in the same severe tone.

'I did wonder if there's some fund I could tap in order to start a small library for the children—adventure and fairy stories and do-it-yourself books. Perhaps the public library would help us. I know in some towns they lend books to the Children's Ward and swop them round every few months.'

'And the committee is to appoint a ward librarian next?'

'Oh, no! I thought one of the older children would enjoy——'

She broke off short, realizing he was just being sarcastic.

'And all this is to be discussed over coffee at the Gannets' when we've sorted out the indoor gardening and the pictures on the ceiling?'

Sheila bit her lip. 'All right, it *is* something I want to discuss with the Chief. I'm sure he'll find ways and means.' Then, looking at him hard: 'Of course, if you were always running away from school I can't expect you to see the point in all this.'

'It was my dream, but I have to confess I never brought it off,' said Red gravely. 'They did hammer the three Rs into me. I can read and write, you know. Somehow I struggled through my medical books. And

I'm in the queue for *Yarns of the Merchant Navy* when Stephen has finished with it.'

He made her feel so foolish! Just when she was about to march off with all the dignity she could muster, he burst out laughing.

'Forgive me. You're doing great things for these children and I oughtn't to rag you.' He put a hand on her arm to detain her and bent his head with its dark flame of hair. 'It's too bad Mrs Gannet has put us off till next week. Quite honestly, to meet right away from the hospital is something—after life in the Residency. I look forward to a rare old set-to over all these schemes you and the Chief are hatching up together. When we do get down to it, don't take it too hard if I make it my business to point out the snags, will you?'

'Saturday night was right *out* for Sheila, anyway. She has a date,' said Ilse Devon's voice close beside them. She used Sheila's first name in a natural, friendly way, but there was some undercurrent, a wariness, as her glance flickered between the two of them.

'I'd forgotten,' said Red, frowning.

There was a momentary pause. Once again Sheila was being offered the chance to mention Victor Cort's appearance at the variety theatre, but she panicked away from it. She was absolutely sure they'd come down like a ton of bricks on her idea of reuniting Gino with his father. Red had made that plain already.

Ilse was smiling up at him now.

'I don't suppose Mrs Gannet put off her invitation for *our* sakes—no matter what we have lined up. It's just that the Swiss pictures aren't ready!'

Well, so that was that. She had conveyed very neatly that other people besides Sheila had a Saturday date. Sheila felt a painful embarrassment. She didn't need any hint from Nurse Porson that there was something between these two, some private relationship—a bond from the past, a promise for the future? She was tinglingly aware of it whenever she saw them together.

And yet, when Red was helping her to pick up her scattered papers and talking about the invitation to Dr Gannet's home, his smile, everything about his manner, had conveyed the idea that he was heartwhole, unattached and often lonely, there in his bachelor quarters at the Residency. And Ilse's manner hinted just the opposite! It made Sheila feel so ill at ease that she searched about for an excuse to slip away and leave them together.

Just then the corridor lights began flashing the Registrar's special combination and off he went with long strides. Ilse disappeared into the heart unit and Sheila went back to the store-room to put away her things till Monday morning.

She found Red just admitting a new case, a haemophiliac. It was a young Austrian boy on a holiday visit. A slight accident had started his bleeding and the doctor his friends called in had rushed him straight to hospital in his own car.

Bang goes the weekend for everyone, Sheila thought. No matter how short-staffed Sister Bain was, she'd have to allocate a nurse to stay constantly with the child till they got the bleeding to stop and were satisfied with his condition, which would be several days, in all probability. Dick Sawley would be keeping watch over him, too, making the tests and managing the transfusions. And Red would be simply run off his feet, keeping in touch with the path lab and organizing the supply of blood and the 'clotting' serum. If it was a severe case, it would mean getting supplies from the regional centre or even further afield.

'No let-up for old Red,' was how Dick Sawley put it, when he met Sheila on Saturday evening. 'A lot of use that filthy great Jag is to him! And if someone had a weekend jaunt in mind'—he looked at Sheila sideways and grinned impishly—'she won't half be mad!' leaving Sheila to guess who he meant. Which, she reflected bleakly, wasn't difficult!

She said quickly: ' How is the case shaping?'

' Tricky. There's the language difficulty. It isn't easy to get sense out of the laddie, and though he has his card with him—details of his past troubles and treatments—that's a headache for the Boss Man, too.' He pulled a face. ' Medical handwriting—in German, and most of it in initials and shortened words. Wow! Red sure has plenty to go at, any time he comes up for air! Jolly decent of him to let me loose for an hour or two.'

Sheila gave him a startled look. ' You—you didn't tell him——'

' About our date? I did, too. And I bet that helped a lot. Gosh, I wouldn't have liked to let you down! As it is, I didn't intend giving you a snack in some ropey little café.'

' It's fun,' Sheila said stoutly.

Dick had had to cut it so fine, their ' slap-up dinner ' was ruled out. He had met her outside the theatre and hurried her across the dingy side-street to a small restaurant almost exactly opposite the stage door. It was kept by a Turkish Cypriot, a large, flabby, pallid man with enormous whiskers. The coffee was wonderful. They ate salad sandwiched between hamburgers and with a hint of strange spices; then they were tempted by the stuffed green walnuts and the Turkish pastries bursting with mint and currants. Sheila ate simply to give Dick pleasure. He had meant it to be such a splendid evening, but it was turning out hasty and makeshift. And she felt ashamed because from her point of view it wasn't what he understood by a ' date '. It was a chance she had seized of getting him to see Victor Cort. Dick, at least, she must win over to her plan. . . . But somehow that made her feel so mean. She hated to think what he had told Red!

She was wound up like a tight spring with suspense and eagerness. But Dick's thoughts were all of practical things: that table at the Plaza he had had to cancel,

Red's Jaguar wasting away in the garage as they left the café and struggled, heads down, against the wind and rain with the gutters of the dark little street running noisily and a cat mewing in a doorway. They had stayed too long over their coffee and hamburgers, and now, if they didn't look sharp, they were going to miss the grand tuning up. 'Best bit of the show, I shouldn't wonder!' grinned Dick.

He hadn't even time or interest to look at the billboards, for he had to leave his name and their seat numbers with the girl at the cash box, in case the hospital called him.

'What did I tell you?' The lights were down already and the orchestra furiously attacking the overture, as they were shown to their 'futtles'. In the dark, Dick bought a programme and a box of chocolates.

'Dick, how sweet of you, but you shouldn't have.'

'Just you wait. Next time we have a date, I'm really going to show you the town!' His hand groped for hers. 'Let it be soon. Promise me . . . my very next free Saturday——'

Poor lad, he really had no luck. She firmly put the programme into his hands; and just so that there'd be no mistake about it, she said it wasn't fair to promise anything with the Chief's coffee party in the offing. He scarcely had time to protest when the usherette was back, flashing her little lamp.

'Doctor Sawley? You're urgently wanted at the hospital.'

'That tears it!' He was the picture of woe. 'I suppose it was too much to hope for a couple of hours off! Can you forgive me?'

'Forgive you! That child needs you, Dick. *Hurry!*'

'Sheila, you're a darned good sport. No other girl would understand, as you do.'

But wasn't it for a child's sake that she herself was here?

She had no chance to tell Dick that now. He thrust

the programme back at her, squeezing her fingers hard, then disappeared up the aisle.

The trick cyclists opened the bill—all red silk tunics and a glitter of chromium, whistling and shouting as they raced about the stage, their legs going madly on the pedals, so that they appeared like fantastic insects cavorting in a beam of sunlight, while the band spanked out the 'Skaters' Waltz'. For Sheila it all merged in a jumble of noise and movement, like the goings-on of the main ward when she was trying to teach the balcony children. After the cyclists the tap-dancing comedian, then a pair of little blonde birds, their heads close together as they warbled into the microphone in small, breathy voices; then the juggler with his merry patter, and the swing group who were top-heavy on the drums and brass. . . .

The whole thing jarred so stridently on her tensed-up mood that she wanted to shut her eyes and cover her ears; and that made her ashamed, for they worked so hard. 'The Fun and Laughter Show' was giving of its Saturday night best to a full house. . . .

She did actually close her eyes. The sudden frenzied applause jerked them open again. The rhythm group had been joined by a fiddler—and that, Sheila knew, was an unfashionable thing, these days. But what a fiddler! Under his bow, the strings leapt to crazy life. You'd have to be deaf as a post and stuffed with wood shavings instead of flesh and blood not to feel your head nodding, your feet tapping, to that beat. You forgot the group, though they were hard at it in the background, drumming, blaring, twanging. All you really heard—and not just with your ears but your whole body —was that fiddler.

The lights clicked. They suddenly dimmed out the rhythm group and Victor Cort was alone at the front of the stage with a spotlight on him. If there had been any doubt in Sheila's mind, it was gone now. This could only be Gino's father—this youngish, dark-haired man, thin to the point of gauntness, wearing a maroon velvet jacket and fantastic, floppy bow-tie, and with dark eyes sunk like pits in a narrow, white face. Even at a distance, across the footlights, she could feel, as she felt it with Gino, the smouldering ill-will of a creature who had always had it tough and felt every man's hand was against him.

She knew what to expect; she'd been amused and touched by the cleaning lady's description of how he brought the whole audience under his spell. She'd be curious to see just how he did it. But now her heart gave a lurch. He had taken another easy step or two forward. He was looking straight at her and playing for her alone: playing his wild gipsy music. The bow seemed to leap under his fingers. He played with savage brilliance. It was wild and gay, love music; then as he drew his bow across the strings in passionate double-stoppings, it was the cry of loneliness and heartbreak, then again a haunting melody, melting and intangible like something half remembered from a dream.

His music wove a spell round her, flowed over her like a tumult of waters, made her shiver with delight and brought an ache of tears to her throat.

Then he was standing with his bow down, bending his head slightly in acknowledgement of the applause, and she caught his smile—contemptuous and weary. They were going crazy all round her, standing up, stamping, calling; and he stood there, a lonely figure with that smile on his lips. The whole thing was an illusion. With the spotlight on him, he couldn't really see them, of course. They were just a blur. And he had been playing for his own pleasure, not theirs. . . .

The curtain swished down, the house lights blazed and the band struck up a Sousa march. It was the interval and the men were jostling towards the bar. Sheila came out of the spell to find herself stumbling up the aisle. It was only the interval and all the turns would be repeated in the second half, but she couldn't take any more. If she gave Dick Sawley a thought at all it was to realize that he wouldn't be free again to-night. He'd be stuck with the new transfusion; and in addition to the haemophiliac child he had other cases to keep him busy right through into the early hours of tomorrow.

She found herself in the side-street, in the bitter sleety rain. She felt dazed and queer. She had seen him, heard him. A mere name had become an intense reality. She had just been through an experience she would never forget. *And NOW what?*

After the overheated little theatre, the chilly rain seemed to strike through her body. She was shivering. Almost automatically she crossed the street and pushed open the door of the little restaurant. The smell of hot fried food almost drove her out again. And then she saw Victor Cort sitting alone at a small table with coffee and soup and some thick, crusty bread in front of him. The place was nearly empty at this hour. There was a couple quarrelling over their meal in the far corner, and a swarthy man smoking some villainous foreign tobacco at the counter, and chatting in a desultory way to the Turk. Sheila's feet mechanically took her across to the counter. The proprietor considered her out of shrewd black eyes.

'Coffee again? Is good, no? Your friend comes soon, eh? That makes two coffees?'

'Just one.' Involuntarily her eyes went to Victor Cort.

The fat Turk nodded and winked.

'So.' He waved a hand. 'Take seat, please. I bring it across.'

She opened her lips to protest, but he was busy already at the espresso machine bubbling and steaming away at the other end of the counter. Without her volition her feet took her across the room, and she stood hesitating near Victor Cort's table. How thin he was! It was the thinness that goes with intense nervous energy—and a wandering life, irregular meals, queer hours, Sheila thought. His face was all jutting angles, and the eyes so deep-set that they were like dark bruises in the pallor of the face. Then suddenly he looked up and the whole face came alive with a sort of angry, smouldering power, exactly as Gino's did. The likeness was heart-wrenching.

The proprietor was at Sheila's elbow. He plonked down a cup of coffee.

'Young lady to see you, Mr Cort. Been in before. Friend of mine, see?' And he winked slyly.

Victor Cort scowled—but *exactly* like Gino!—and made an impatient gesture with his hand.

'Autograph? Where's your book?' As she shook her head, he frowned again. 'No autograph book. Then you want me to hear you play your fiddle.' He reached out, with that insolent, impatient gesture, and seized her right hand, gave it a look and dropped it. 'No corns. That means no fiddle. What *do* you play?'

The Turk had gone back to the counter and turned his back, continuing his conversation with the swarthy man, who puffed out smoke like an old tramp steamer.

'Well?' Victor Cort said impatiently.

Now that she was face to face with him, Sheila felt so paralysed with nervousness that she had to make a supreme effort to speak at all.

'As a matter of fact, I play the guitar. But that's not——'

'Oh, God! Don't you know that kids with guitars come ten a penny, these days? You've got to have a gimmick. And even then it's just a question of luck. Either you send them or you make them sick. . . . If you're after a telly audition, I can't help you.'

And he went back to his soup and bread as if that closed the interview.

Sheila dropped into the chair opposite him, her fingers crisping hard on the edge of the table. Suddenly she felt so *angry*.

'I don't try to get by, strumming three chords on a

horrible electric machine. Mine is a Spanish guitar and I really can play it. But the last thing in the world I want is an audition for television. It isn't about music that I'm here. It's about Gino.'

He went on crumbling bread and taking soup as if he hadn't heard.

'Gino,' Sheila repeated, her voice cracking. 'Your little boy.'

He didn't look up, but slowly he put down his spoon. After a measurable pause in which Sheila seemed to hear her own heart thudding, he raised his head. His eyes were dark, opaque, they told her nothing. But his voice said harshly: 'Who the hell are you?'

'I'm Sheila Thorne. I work at the hospital—I'm the ward teacher—and we've got Gino there. He's had a long illness. And the Browns——' Her voice gave out. That stony stare of his put her off. She drew a shaking breath and stumbled on: 'I know I'm sticking my neck out. This isn't really my business. But . . . but you see, I love Gino.'

That was true. She knew it suddenly. A lost little boy who lived shut into some fantasy world of his own was always there in the back of her thoughts, no matter what else she was doing, who she was with. For his sake she would, she *must*, risk everything. As she was risking everything now.

She repeated in a painful whisper: 'It isn't my business. Perhaps it's the almoner's business. Or nobody's business. But I had to tell you. Because the Browns——'

But what could she tell him about the Browns, whom she'd never even seen? Just her fears, her suspicions, because with her own eyes she saw what they had made of that child. She hesitated, in an agony of indecision, and looked at him mutely, a terrible urgency in her eyes. He was very white, his face glistening with sweat—or was it his stage make-up?

He stood up, pushing back his chair with a hideous

scraping sound. His soup was only half finished, his coffee untouched.

He said harshly: 'You're making a mistake. I have no child.'

And then, with long violent strides, he was gone, and the door flapped after him.

The Turk waddled across, shaking his head sympathetically.

'So many young ladies wait at the stage door, you understand?' He shrugged and threw out his hands. 'Years and years he is playing his violin and no one wants to listen. Then two minutes on telly and that does the trick. But how long it lasts? That's another thing again, no?'

She was out in the street, in the rain and the dark, walking, walking.... She had never before been in this old quarter of the city at night. The warehouses and office blocks were looming dark shapes, then came a row of brightly lit shop-fronts, past which people hurried through the rain. At the pub on the corner they were making a lively shindy. A policeman stood across the street, his cape streaming with wet. Then there were hoardings, above which, at a distance, she could see the hospital lights.

The ugly, dingy red brick was gone, there were only the lights, comforting and kindly. She felt a great rush of thankfulness for this place that never slept. It made her think of a ship on a dark ocean and she wanted to send up a prayer for all who sailed in her: the night nurses, the lab technician working all night for the sake of the little Austrian boy, Dick Sawley watching the transfusion, and Red making his late round, like the officer of the watch....

She only realized now that ever since she left the little restaurant, her feet had been leading her here: to the hospital, to Red. She had to see him. It was crazy at this hour, but she had to see him. He would be angry, too, that she had gone seeking out Gino's father: had thrust herself on to him and told him about the child.

And that had led nowhere, after all. She would never forget those dark, shuttered eyes. 'You're making a mistake. I have no child.' What a mockery that made of the wild, passionate music he drew from his violin: music that could charm the soul out of you. . . .

Red would say: 'I told you so,' and she could take that meekly. At least she had put her dream to the test, it wouldn't go on haunting her. She would listen to Red and the almoner now and try to accept what they planned for the child's future.

She came out of these whirling thoughts suddenly. A dog's lead was tangled round her legs. It was a little black poodle wearing a comical red jacket. It exactly matched the red nylon raincoat of a slim woman who was exercising the dog in the rain. She wore a scarf over dark hair and she had bent with a murmur of apology to sort out the tangled lead before Sheila recognized her. It was Ilse Devon.

Straightening up, she saw Sheila's face.

'Why, Sheila, my dear! This is a surprise! Walking all alone in the rain?' Her smile changed to a look of concern. 'What's wrong?'

'Nothing,' gulped Sheila. 'Nothing at all.'

'You're absolutely drenched. Not even a rain-hood.'

Sheila put up a hand to her hair in a dazed sort of way.

'I'm all right.' Her face broke up. 'Only I've made such an awful fool of myself.'

'Your date——' began Ilse. Then she gave a little wry smile, as if she understood perfectly. She took Sheila's arm in a firm, friendly grasp. 'There isn't a dry inch on you! I wouldn't turn a dog out on such a night! . . . Except that Treena absolutely insisted on a trot round the block. I think we timed it very nicely, don't you?'

Sheila resisted her hand. 'I'm all right, really I am.' She could have wept. She had been so near the hospital, so near Red. . . .

Ilse said firmly: 'I'm taking you home with me.'

CHAPTER VII

Sheila felt too far gone in misery even to protest. Ilse's hand on her arm hurried her down a crooked little street overshadowed by the shop-fronts and office buildings. It brought them out into a quiet residential square. On one side there were trees in a railed garden, and facing this a terrace of well-kept, old-fashioned houses with areas and imposing front steps. The little dog, let off the lead, pranced ahead of them, its black tail upheld like a brush, its body waggling in the comical red flannel jacket, and ran up the steps of the third house in the row, which had two brass plates on the door.

Ilse took Sheila straight upstairs, inserted her key in a door on the landing, and they were in a little cream-painted hall with a glowing amethyst carpet flowing over it like a 'wine-dark sea'. From where she stood Sheila could glimpse other rooms of the flat through half-open doors. It was all very spacious and uncluttered, done in simple lines and vivid colours in an elegant modern style. Just what Sheila would have expected after seeing Ilse's office in the physiotherapy department.

She said in distress: 'I'm dripping on your lovely carpet.' A shaky laugh came out. 'I feel like the King of the Golden River, simply dissolving away! And I'd hardly even noticed it was raining——'

'It just goes to show,' said Ilse, shocked. 'Don't worry about the carpet, it's terribly hard-wearing. I've been wanting an excuse for a new one for ages, and not a hope! Here.'

She held out a hand for Sheila's coat, having already shed her own jewel-bright outer layer, under which she wore a short black cocktail dress. It was obvious that Sheila was wet to the skin. She suddenly began sneezing violently.

'Someone ought to give you a good shaking for getting in such a state,' said Ilse. 'I've nursed Treena through pneumonia this winter—and we don't want to start with you!'

Sheila took an uncertain step towards the lounge, but Ilse quickly spun her round in the opposite direction.

'In here! Off with those wet things!'

It was almost as if she wanted to prevent her seeing into the lounge; but Sheila had already glimpsed a decanter and sherry glasses set out on a beautiful little silver tray, and away to one side a low coffee table with an electric hotplate, cups and plates for two, and a luscious chocolate cake dusted with icing sugar. Ilse couldn't have foreseen her visit, and certainly she didn't make such preparations on the offchance! She was expecting someone. Suddenly and desperately Sheila wanted to escape. But, as with the hall carpet, not a hope!

Ilse was thrusting towels and a silk quilted housecoat into her arms and showing her into a tiny, beautifully appointed bathroom in which everything but the towels and bathmat was pure white.

'It's minute,' Ilse apologized. 'Not even room for a bath! I had a shower fitted instead. I took a slice off the original bathroom—Victorian, a real museum piece—and tacked it on to a small bedroom to make my kitchen. I adore cooking and I must have space for it.'

Sheila thought of the chocolate cake and wondered what savoury dish was to appear on the hotplate. If only she could forget that hateful remark of Nurse Porson's about the Black Widow spider and the parlour!

'Chuck out your wet things and I'll dry them while you're having a hot drink,' said Ilse, shutting the bathroom door on her.

The shower was heavenly, the towels thick and luxurious. There were skin lotions and perfumes and powders on the shelf at which Ilse had waved a hand, inviting her to use anything she liked. But she towelled in haste, slipped on the housecoat over her underwear and came out of the steamy fragrance resolved not to intrude on Ilse's Saturday evening a moment longer than necessary.

There was a coffee pot on the hotplate and Ilse was at the window, staring out and smoking a cigarette. Sheila went over and joined her.

'You've been so kind. I'll clear off as soon as my things are dry.'

'There's no rush,' said Ilse, turning with a smile that she had to switch on with an effort. 'I'm going to lace your coffee with rum in the true sailor's fashion. Come over to the fire.'

But Sheila lingered at the window a moment longer. Through curtains of rain she saw the garden in the square, with bulbs flowering under the trees whose branches were tossed roughly by the bitter wind. Under the street-lamps the green of the trees was pale and unnatural, almost like cardboard trees on a stage set, and it seemed uncanny to see the branches bend and the leaves flutter. And beyond and above them shone the lights of the hospital. Was that where Ilse's glance had rested? *There's no rush.* . . . Because, of course, the little Austrian boy had wrecked her Saturday date, too. And that walk round the block hadn't just been for the poodle's sake but to work off her fed-upness.

As she went over to the fireplace, Sheila said: 'This house . . . the square . . . it's such a surprise. In the heart of the city!'

'A G.P. has to live near his patients. Plenty of doctors' wives have to start married life in a creaking old house, all cellars and attics, in some drab street. Mark and I might have done worse, I suppose.'

'Your husband . . . practised here?' asked Sheila carefully. She had the feeling that the topic of Ilse Devon's marriage was very thin ice indeed.

'Oh, yes. And he had great plans. It was to be a multiple practice eventually, with three or four good names on the plate. You see, the City Council changed their minds about making this a scheduled area and began building workers' flats instead. That meant customers on our doorstep, and the hospital so handy if Mark had to refer patients there for X-rays and that sort of thing. I must say M.G.H. gives the family doctor more facilities than some hospitals. Oh, yes, wonderful plans!' She laughed on a breaking note. 'That six-wheeler lorry put paid to it all.' Over her coffee cup she gave Sheila a swift glance. 'You've heard the whole story by now, I'm sure.'

Sheila shook her head. Her eyes held distress and pity. Ilse gave that strident laugh again.

'What, not even from the Porson? She's the eyes and ears of Marbury General. Nothing misses her. And she's running to that unspeakable uncle with every little bit of gossip she hears.' That was said bitterly, almost savagely. She offered a box of cigarettes. Sheila refused one and she lit her own with a hand that shook, inhaled deeply, and said through the drift of smoke: 'Mark was on his rounds one morning. He was getting out of his car at a patient's house. This big lorry came too close and caught him. He died in the ambulance.'

Sheila could find no words. The story was shocking, terrible. The tragic waste. . . .

Ilse echoed her thought: 'The dreadful, dreadful waste. He'd only been in practice a couple of years and he wasn't very businesslike about accounts. And of course, these days, you can't sell the goodwill of a practice, the Medical Executive just appoints someone to take over. The legal wrangling over insurance and compensation dragged on and on. A nightmare. The lorry-driver claimed Mark was negligent. Though of course it was just the other way round. The thing isn't really settled yet.'

She was walking rapidly up and down, flinging words over her shoulder in little jerky phrases.

'Dr Gannet saw to it that I got my job back. I'd given it up when I married Mark. And when I decided to stay on in this house, there was the headache of getting planning permission. In the end, all the form-filling and the arguing gets you down. I wanted to turn this floor into a flat for myself, shut off the attics and rent off the ground floor as consulting-rooms. Two of the big bods from the hospital share it, and it works out rather well.' Again that bitter, disillusioned laugh. ' Of course it's their money I'm after. A girl has to live, and I charge them the highest rent I dare.'

' And you've made this flat beautiful,' said Sheila, glancing round with sincere pleasure.

' Oh, it's all right for the time being,' said Ilse. She threw the half-smoked cigarette into the fire, glanced at her watch, moved about the room restlessly—drew the curtains, cut Sheila a slice of chocolate cake, switched on the television. Always she had seemed poised and mistress of herself; but tonight her nerves had raw edges and she couldn't hide it. She slipped out. To remove from the heat whatever she had cooking, Sheila thought, then realized that she was telephoning. Above the television which Ilse had turned up loud she could make out the click and purr of the telephone dial and the low murmur of her voice.

After a delay of a few moments which seemed to stretch out to snapping point, Ilse heard the voice she hoped for. But it was a voice making excuses.

' Look, Ilse, I'm sorry to let you down, but it's just been impossible to get away. Before I can leave young Sawley to cope with the transfusion, I must check on the latest count from the path lab.'

' You're near enough! Can't you slip along for half an hour—coffee and a bite of something hot?'

' That business we have to discuss will take more than half an hour! Better leave it till I have a good long evening free.'

Ilse bit her lip. ' Damn the business,' she said raggedly. That was a mistake; she knew it the instant the words were out; tried to cover it with a little laugh. ' Red darling, it's dragged on so long, what's a week more or less? I'm thinking of *you* now. You absolutely neglect yourself. The coffee smells heavenly, I wish I could waft it to you over the wire. It'd bring you like a shot!'

Red laughed shortly. 'They brew up tea and coffee alternately in the kitchen of this ward all night long! Sorry, Ilse, but you see how it is. Of course, if the blood count and pressure reading are what I hope . . . The lab may ring me any moment.'

'Is that a polite way of telling me to get off the line?'

'Now, look here——'

'Not that I'm lonely,' Ilse said recklessly. 'Guess who? Our little friend Sheila Thorne, whom I found wandering about in the rain, soaked through and in a distressed state. Really far gone.'

Dead silence at the other end.

Then Red growled: 'But hang it all, she knows Dick has his hands full here.'

'Ah!' Ilse said swiftly. 'So it *is* Dick Sawley! You know, darling, the girl's deep. She told me she wasn't interested in boys!'

But she was talking to herself: Red had rung off.

Poised, confident, quite her old self, she went back to the lounge, peered into the coffee pot, then settled herself gracefully in a big chair and smiled across at her guest.

'Feeling better? Yes, your colour has come back. Just relax. And if there's anything you want to get off your mind, Sheila, my dear, now's your chance. I'm your friend. And a trouble shared, you know . . . Do confide in me!'

While she was out of the room Sheila had been resolving to do that very thing. She was absolutely disillusioned about Victor Cort: the temperamental musician who meant to get to the top at any price, whose head was turned by one little television appearance; the man who rejected his own child. If Ilse had kept silent then, she would have found courage to bring out her hopes, her disappointment, her anguish about Gino's future. But she was too impatient. She leaned forward a little and said teasingly: 'Is it really such a dreadful thing when a date lets you down?'

Sheila looked at her with a sort of surprise.

'Oh, it was only Dick—and he didn't let me down. We—we had seats for the theatre and the show had only just started when he was called out. But we half expected that. Probably he had to put up another transfusion for the little Austrian boy.'

Ilse was genuinely startled—and intensely curious. It showed in her eyes, in the way she suddenly leaned forward.

'Then it was something that happened after Dick left you? Now you've really got me guessing!' The girl's eyes were wide with distress, her face so flushed. She looked absurdly young in the firelight, the folds of the lovely housecoat falling round her slim figure. Yes, young and innocent. Ideas flashed through her mind: Saturday night, tipsy revellers in the street, a pretty girl hurrying past alone; a drunk jostling her, perhaps, or calling out something foul. Half teasing, half serious, she suggested: 'Sheila dear, is it a matter for the police?'

The effect on Sheila was startling. She sprang to her feet.

'Oh, no. No! That's the last thing. . . . It would make it all ten times worse!'

Why hadn't she thought of that? If it was true that Gino had never been legally adopted by the Browns because the parent's signature was essential and Victor Cort couldn't be traced, they or the almoner might seek to take that step now, with the help of the police. He would sign away the child willingly enough, it seemed to her. But if the Browns had really made up their minds not to have him back, that would pin the care of him fairly and squarely on his father, who had stared at her in that frightening way this very evening and said:

'You're making a mistake. I have no child.' Oh, better, far better, that he should be under the care of the public authority in a well-run Home.

She had so nearly betrayed the child she loved. And Ilse would dig it all out of her in five minutes if she stayed. In a panic to be away, she threw off the housecoat, slipped the little blue nylon dress over her head. 'Nylon is wonderful! This is perfectly dry already. And my stockings.' Her shoes were still sodden and Ilse could lend her none of the right size, but it didn't matter—she'd quickly be home. Ilse insisted on calling a taxi; and so urgent was Sheila's haste to be gone, she had thanked Ilse for all her kindness and was waiting on the steps when the taxi rolled up.

And only just in time. As they drove out of the square, Red's black and silver Jaguar passed them. Peering through the rear window, Sheila saw him stop outside the third house, caught the blaze of his hair under the doorlight as he took the front steps in big strides.

How thankful Ilse must be that she hadn't stayed longer! Her heart gave a queer little lurch as she pictured the low coffee table, firelight glancing off the silver things, the big inviting chairs.

The thing she didn't see was Timothy Redfern's expression as Ilse greeted him.

'Red darling, this is wonderful. I know you're worn out and famished. I'll dish up in just two minutes. You've just missed Sheila. Something's wrong there, but I couldn't coax it out of her. Like I told you, darling, the girl's deep——'

* * *

The most hectic weekend ever, was the report Sheila got on Monday morning. A run on the blood bank for the little Austrian boy, whom they were planning to fly home as soon as it was safe; the Chief popping in and out without warning; Red on the rampage.

'And on top of that,' confided Nurse Connell, 'this

terrible wild fellow turning up and claiming he'd be Gino's father.'

Sheila's heart gave that lurch again. Had she misjudged Victor Cort, after all?

'Did they . . . take to one another?' She held her breath as she waited for the staff nurse's answer.

Eileen Connell looked at her sideways.

'They didn't let him see the boy. Sister kept him in her office and sent round a call for the Boss Man. And the both of them soon sent him packing.'

'Oh, *no!*' whispered Sheila, aghast.

After that she seemed to be walking about in a daze. She was tied by lessons all morning and Sister was busy with admissions from the Outpatient clinic. It was after lunch before Sheila got to see her. Facing her across the little office, she blurted: 'I was told Gino's father came in to see him and that he wasn't allowed . . . that you and Doctor Redfern——' Tears sprang to her eyes and she let fly regardless. 'How could you be so cruel?'

'How would you have handled it?' snapped Sister Bain. 'There's been no sight or sound of him for eight years. He suddenly turns up and demands to see the child, talks wildly of his legal rights and challenges the Registrar's authority to keep him out.' She looked thoughtful. 'If there was no regular adoption, he certainly has legal rights. Unfortunately.' Sheila made a little wincing movement, and Sister Bain saw it and challenged her. 'We're not disputing he's the father. The likeness is quite startling. But what is this going to mean for Gino?'

Sheila had done some painful thinking on that subject, too, during the weekend. She said: 'The Browns moved away from Edgware a long time ago. Mr Cort may have tried to get in touch with the child before now and not succeeded.'

'Quite, quite!' Red's voice made her jump. He was in the office doorway. 'The mystery is, why should he turn up at the hospital at the end of a month's run of some cheap show he's touring in? Why yesterday? Why not earlier? And how did he know we had the child here?'

Sheila steadied herself for the wrath to come.

'I told him.'

She heard Sister gasp. Red said nothing. He gave her a strange, unquiet look.

'It's really too bad keeping us in the dark, Miss Thorne!' A spot of Dutch-doll colour burned in Sister Bain's cheeks. 'Not a word to *anyone*!'

'Perhaps,' said Red, 'there hasn't been time.' He frowned over the thing. 'Admittedly, the Browns can't have tried very hard to track him down. He's appearing in public.' His mouth twisted. 'And he doesn't strike me as the bloke to go hiding his light under a bushel.'

'They thought he'd gone abroad,' said Sister. 'I asked Mrs Brown—without letting on that he'd been here.' She coughed. 'I thought we'd better leave all that to the almoner.'

The Registrar looked at Sheila under his brows. His gaze was hard and disconcerting.

'By an odd coincidence we've had Mrs Brown here, too. You don't by any chance know something about that?'

'She's with Gino now,' said Sister Bain.

'I think Miss Thorne should meet her, Sister.'

'Very well, Doctor,' said Sister resignedly, seeing her off-duty fly out at the window. 'Nurse Connell is getting Norina ready for you.'

'Right,' he said briskly.

Sheila was aware that he stood there, frowning and thoughtful, watching them go down the ward and out to the balcony. Sister said over her shoulder: 'The Chief got on to a new treatment for Norina's type of anaemia at that congress. What with her blood-tests and the transfusions for Franzl we're keeping the lab busy. And then the new admissions. And Mrs Brown on top of all that!'

She was a thin woman with straggly fair hair, vague

features, vague blue eyes and a pouting mouth. Nothing you could get hold of and pin down, Sheila found herself thinking. But she dismissed once and for all the idea that she had physically ill-treated Gino. No, it would all be vaguer—or more subtle—than that. She was sitting by the bed and Gino was pretending she wasn't there, while around them the other children chattered and called out to one another.

'This is Miss Thorne, the ward teacher,' said Sister Bain. And with a little nod she left them together.

'Well, I hope you can get some sense out of the child. He has us whacked,' said Mrs Brown. 'We've tried everything, honest we have. Well, see for yourself! He won't even look at what I brought him.'

She had brought along a picture book for a much younger child and a teddy-bear still in its plastic wrappings.

'It's our Alec's birthday. Yes, he was three yesterday, and that's why I came along. To bring Gino a slice of birthday cake and a balloon, and you'd think that'd cheer him up a bit, wouldn't you?'

The slice of iced cake in a paper serviette confirmed Sheila's guess that the picture book and the teddy-bear had been meant for someone else, and hastily switched to Gino. Would the reason for that be an item in the *Marbury Gazette* about the 'Fun and Laughter Show' —or was it that one brief moment on the telly which someone had happened to mention to the Browns? It stood out a mile that she hadn't yielded to a sudden loving impulse. *The woman was afraid.* She cried a little when Gino wouldn't speak to her, and the other children stopped their chatter and watched with clinical interest. Any minute now Gino would start swearing.

Sheila told them to get on with their sums and hastily showed Mrs Brown out. She mopped at her eyes.

'It's hard, when you've done everything for a child. A month old he was when Mr Cort left him with us, and we treated him just like he was our own. Mind you, he had his little ways even as a baby. Fly into a rage he would, over something and nothing, when he was only two years old. And later . . . This toy fiddle someone gave him at Christmas, and he was sawing away at it all day long. We couldn't even get him to the table for his meals, and Mr Brown was that provoked, he threw the thing in the ashbin. That was no cause for the child to take on so—cry himself sick and refuse his food. We could see what he'd be like if music really took a hold on him. We meant it for the best, Miss Thorne, we did really.'

Behind them, Gino blew up the balloon with ferocious resolution till it burst with a loud pop. In a way, that was swearing, thought Sheila!

Mrs Brown said tearfully: 'I must have been a bit hard-pressed when I said we didn't want him back. But Sister knows I never meant it. We'll come for him just as soon as the doctor says the word. Tell him that, won't you?'

Sheila, stiff and pale, said: 'It's not for me to tell him anything. You'd better see the almoner. Sister Bain will arrange that. Good afternoon, Mrs Brown.'

They had thrown his toy violin in the ashbin. And what had they told him about his father, about worthless, no-good musicians, about their own mistake in taking a nobody's child into their home? She wanted to weep at the thought of Gino going back to them. And the alternative she had dreamt of seemed hopeless.

The rain had cleared up during the day and she came out of the hospital to pale, relenting skies and a sudden tenderness of spring again in the air.

As she came through the archway a waiting figure stepped to meet her. He was haggard and pale, the collar of a once-smart overcoat turned up, his dark hair in a careless tangle.

'Miss Thorne,' he greeted her.

'I—I thought you were miles away by now,' stammered Sheila. 'At the other side of the Pennines.'

'We open in Sheffield tonight. I skipped the run-through and you know I'm not on stage till just before the interval. I'm cutting it fine. My train leaves in exactly an hour. I must talk to you.'

Sheila said, as she had said to Mrs Brown: 'You'd better talk to the almoner.'

He ignored that. He had grasped her by the elbow and was urging her towards the pavement edge, where he began snapping his fingers for a taxi.

'The almoner!' he repeated savagely. 'If anyone in the world can help me, it's you.'

'Mr Cort, I should never have approached you. I—I spoke out of turn. It just isn't my business, and . . .'

A taxi drew up. Before she really knew what was happening, Victor Cort had bundled her into it and she was driving off beside him.

CHAPTER VIII

Tonight it wasn't a hasty hamburger at what Dick Sawley called a 'ropey little café' in a side-street.

Sheila found herself seated opposite Victor Cort in a quiet Italian restaurant where you got a clue to the price-range from the exquisite flower arrangement just inside the door, the snowy table-linen and deft waiters.

They were served with a risotto and a long roll of bread brought to the table still hot, wrapped in a napkin. There was a smooth red wine and a bowl of fruit which the waiter placed on the table and then wished them a good appetite and melted discreetly away. When Sheila protested at the lavish order, Victor said he was trying to make up for the rude brush-off last Saturday.

'Can you understand? I had shut the door on the past and thrown away the key. And there you were, conjuring up ghosts——'

The ghosts were in his eyes as he took her step by step over the wanderings of the years since Gino was born. And then, as memories too long shut away struggled up towards the light, he took her further still: to the little fishing village on the Adriatic coast where he had found himself ten years ago when his ancient Fiat broke down between Acona and Bologna. He was touring with a troupe of Italian musicians, picking up one-night stands where they could. They had an engagement in Milan; the others hired another car and pressed on. Victor threw Milan to the winds and stayed behind. He had fallen in love.

It was the annual festival of the sea, when the priest came right down to the water's edge to bless the tiny fishing fleet which had dwindled to half a dozen or so in late years. In front of the priest went a small surpliced boy ringing a bell, behind him came the choirboys singing, and the festival queen attended by a scared little girl in white, then the whole village in a holiday mood. The sun sent down golden rays that seemed to bless the whole scene, priest and all, and coaxed forth fragrance from the lemon trees and the stone pines, glanced off the sapphire sea and the red rocks and the dazzle of sardine scales caught in the nets spread out to dry. At night there was music. Music everywhere, and laughter and fragrance. . . .

Victor went to the garage where repairs on the old Fiat were held up because of the festival. He took out his fiddle and strolled back in the starlight, all that beauty aching in him, tingling in his fingers. He had come face to face in the village street with the festival queen, in a merry group of girl friends, the little attendant in white tagging after them.

'My Giovanna was seventeen, dark-haired, pale as a dream. They had crowned her with orange flowers, and it made me think of a bridal wreath.'

There in the street he had put his fiddle to his shoulder and lifted his bow and played for her. That was all his wooing. Sheila knew exactly, but *exactly* how it would be. With the spell of his music on her, the girl would have followed him to the ends of the earth. They were never left alone together, Victor said with a little wry twist to his lips. The little sister Bianca was there, big-eyed and sleepy, even when the girl friends, giggling and nudging one another, went back to the merrymaking in the square in front of the church. But everything was confessed and everything promised in the first glance he and Giovanna exchanged.

He had it out with her father, old Peri, who did a coastwise trade from Rimini northwards and southwards, and who didn't care to see his pretty daughter married off to a vagabond player, and a foreigner at that.

'But her mother had a soul for music,' said Victor. And Sheila understood perfectly.

When the old Fiat was ready to take the road a couple of weeks later, Victor's bride went with him. To Milan. And from Milan over the Alps. And at last, at long last, to England. Sheila thought of that strange, rootless life for the young girl from an Adriatic village. The cheap lodgings, the draughty, shabby music halls where she waited for Victor every night in the wings. Occasionally it would be a seaside resort: but a steel-grey English sea under threatening skies, and the rain. . . . And then the baby.

'She'd never been strong, and the climate . . . She had this little rasping cough. It used to get on my nerves. She was starved for the sun. And, God help me, I couldn't take her back. It never ran to it, you know. We just scraped through each week.' His face was a mask of anguish. 'She had the baby, and held him in her arms and loved him. And then she was rambling about the priest's blessing; it was all mixed up with the blessing of the fishing boats at Rimini. They were worried about her temperature and her cough. It was pneumonia. She just slipped away from us, and in a few hours it was over.'

His face was working. And Sheila couldn't have brought out a word to save her life.

'I didn't want the child,' he went on in a rough, jerky voice. 'I wanted Giovanna. But the Browns, where we lodged then, were desperate for a baby. They begged me to leave Gino with them. And with no strings.' Again that wry, tragic grimace that passed for a smile. 'Certainly not violin strings. They wanted the child to have a decent upbringing, a settled home. And I was going about like a man whose heart is in the grave. I'd have agreed to anything. I paid over the money and cleared out.'

Sheila was jerked back to awareness. 'The money?'

'When I brought Giovanna to England I fulfilled one promise I'd made to old Peri. I insured us both. It was her father's idea of security. It was more than we could afford. And I'd rage at the burden when we had to scrape and go hungry to pay what was due. When she died I couldn't grasp at first what the Browns were trying to ram home to me. There was five hundred pounds to come. I couldn't have touched a penny of it, the idea made me want to vomit. . . . But for the child's sake, the Browns kept saying. I gave them the money, the lot. It was my share towards Gino's upbringing. It eased my conscience. I found I could play again. I was grateful—the Browns had made it possible for me to put the past away, to wipe out the whole tragedy and start my life again.' His laugh was a frightening thing. His eyes burned into Sheila's.

'Oh God, if you knew what I feel about that now. But I swear to you that *at the time* I thought I was doing the best thing for Gino. The only thing. A vagabond musician—where would a child have fitted in? And the Browns offering him everything.'

Offering everything—and giving so little. Sheila's heart twisted. It wasn't for her to judge, they might have been sincere, they might have loved the child at the start. Then Brown was tempted to invest in a little business up north—besides the five hundred pounds there'd be the proceeds of their Edgware house; but it was still not enough, or trade was bad, or he was just butter-fingered when it came to handling money. And they had children of their own. That happened time and time again when a childless couple adopted a baby. In Gino's case there wasn't even a legal adoption, just a ' friendly arrangement'. They had seized on that loophole when they asked the hospital almoner about finding another home for Gino.

Then suddenly they had got wind that Victor was in the district. A day of reckoning had loomed up. It had brought Mrs Brown to the hospital in a panic, armed with presents and fair words.

Victor Cort leaned across the table.

' After the show closed on Saturday night I walked the wet streets for hours. The friends who put me up during the run of the show thought I'd got mixed up in a street accident. They were just ringing the police when I walked in. I couldn't even tell them where I'd been. But one thing I knew for sure. You had brought Gino back into my life. He needs me and I need him. Lena and Frank—these friends I just mentioned, they're musicians, too—didn't wake me, I slept twelve hours solid. When I woke they had a meal ready, but I couldn't touch it, I was crazy to get to that child. I went straight to the hospital. It was visiting hour all right, people were streaming in. But when I gave my name to the nurse at the ward doors, she side-tracked me, stuck me in a little office and fetched the Sister in charge. And then this doctor turned up—they'd sent for him, I reckon. A big bully of a chap with red hair. They wouldn't let me see Gino.'

Sheila found she couldn't meet his eyes any more. She groped for the right thing to say. ' You—you have to look at it from their point of view. The child is . . . difficult. And he's been very ill. A surprise like that——'

'He's been ill and he needs me,' Victor said doggedly. His face twisted with sudden passion. She had seen Gino with just the same look. 'If there'd only been the two women in uniform, I'd have gone in—and to hell with their objections. But this clever devil——' There was a glare of hatred in his eyes. 'I haven't finished with him yet. I'll be back, with all the documents to prove my legal rights, and I'll cram them down his throat if he tries to keep me from my son.'

'Mr Cort!'

He saw her horrified look and the rage went out of him. He put up shaking hands to his face.

'I'm sorry. I took the thing very hard. You'd wrenched a door open and let light into the dark places. I went to that place with hope in my heart. Gino would know me. We'd be together. Just now, when my luck has turned at last. . . . He'd share that good fortune with me. . . . Well, I was wrong. I have to leave Marbury without seeing him. But you're *for* me, aren't you, Sheila Thorne? You must be, or you wouldn't have sought me out at the theatre. I'm leaving Gino in your hands.'

He reached across and lifted her hands to his lips. It was a theatrical gesture, yet she also found it humble and touching.

'Talk to Gino about me,' he begged, 'so that when I come back and see him he won't be meeting a stranger.' An idea occurred to him, and he snapped his fingers excitedly. 'Look, they're broadcasting part of the show on Friday night—direct from the theatre. It'll be latish, but you have a pull, you can get permission for Gino to listen in. Yes, that's it. He'll meet me first through my music. I'll be playing just for him.'

The waiter coughed. He was hovering in distress. Their beautiful risotto of prawns and mushrooms was going cold and they had scarcely touched their wine. Victor glanced at his watch and jumped up with an exclamation.

'My train! I'll just make it if I'm lucky with a taxi.' As he grabbed for his sinister-looking black hat with the rakish brim and the old overcoat with a button hanging loose, he laughed aloud, excited and jubilant. 'But this is my lucky day. I'm on the up and up, Sheila Thorne. The tide has turned for me. We have a future ahead of us, Gino and I.' As she began getting to her feet he stopped her with a lordly gesture. 'Enjoy your meal. And listen with Gino, won't you? The "Méditation" from *Thaïs* will be for *you*. It's the thing I love best.'

Again he made that handsome, extravagant gesture with his right hand, as if saluting with a fiddle bow. Then he was gone.

He had left her to pay the bill. She could have wept with rage. It was pure luck that she happened to have enough money on her. And the future was just as vague, as unsettled, as ever it had been for Gino. All the same, she'd have liked to stitch that button on his coat!

* * *

He little guessed, Sheila thought, what a dragon-slaying there must be before she got permission for Gino to hear that broadcast. She tackled her first dragon on Tuesday morning. And a very puny Saint George she felt herself to be as she suggested to Sister Bain that it would be a splendid way for the child to make his father's acquaintance. She saw the first objection coming and added quickly that it needn't disturb the other children. She would bring along a transistor and she and Gino would listen in 'ever so quietly'.

Sister tightened her lips. She was against it, of course. But she merely said she would 'put it up to the Registrar' and changed the subject to a Mrs Jeffreys whose baby was in for a cleft palate operation. She had come in with him in order to feed and nurse him—it was so important that he shouldn't cry—but while he slept she would have time on her hands and it seemed a good idea for Sheila to get her helping with the other children.

'Gladly, Sister! I'll be happy to have an assistant—especially as we're to lose Jackie today.'

Jackie had been marching around announcing proudly: 'I'm stabilized!' As if, Dick Sawley said, he were the *Queen Elizabeth*. They were going to miss him. But perhaps, said Sheila, giving Sister a hopeful look, Gino would be up and about, any time now, and could be her monitor. Could he perhaps help Stephen with the model yacht he was building now?

'He isn't out of the wood yet, and we don't want any setback.' His father barging in and making scenes, for instance, was in Sister's tone. So Sheila didn't press it.

But for her torment of mind over Gino's future, she would have been so happy now. She loved this place. And the problems which had loomed so large were solving themselves beautifully since the Chief came back from Switzerland to back her up. She had her equipment for lessons, the famous 'pictures on the ceiling' projector was on order; they had started a library shelf and one of the bigger girls had fun ruling up a notebook to keep track of the borrowers.

It wouldn't be long before the flowers that bloomed in the spring would bloom for Marbury General, too. Dr Gannet had sent along the hospital carpenter to measure up for window-boxes. It seemed a long wait to the children and perhaps Jackie had chattered about it; for when his parents came to fetch him they brought some little pots of bulbs just coming into flower. And Sister, turning all reckless on her day off, blued some of her precious 'ward money' on packets of easy-to-grow seeds guaranteed to pop out of the soil as if chased by moles and burst forthwith into gorgeous flowers.

Oh, yes, a happy and a busy week; but over it hung Victor Cort's shadow. It wasn't till Friday morning that Red planted himself in front of her as she crossed the ward and said without any beating about the bush: 'So you think Gino ought to meet his father by transistor!'

'Through his music, yes,' said Sheila, resenting the sardonic one-sided smile.

He took his eyes from her and frowned at his thoughts.

'I hoped I'd got rid of the fellow. I can't see him bringing anything but trouble. And the child is mixed-up enough already.'

'You've only heard the Browns' side, Doctor.'

'And you, I take it, have heard Cort's.' He frowned again. 'He undoubtedly has legal rights. He can sort that out with the foster-parents. Thank God it isn't our affair.' He hunched his shoulders. 'Very well, if he's going to stick around we shall have to give him access to the child. And if you can put it over in some way that this stranger is in fact his nearest and dearest—good luck to you.'

Sheila had to lower her eyes. They betrayed such pain and anger. Above her head she heard the Registrar say in a gruff, abrupt voice: 'Sorry I wrecked your Saturday date by calling Sawley in. Ilse tells me you were upset about it. Again—I'm sorry. But it's just one of those things.'

How far he was from understanding! Watching him stride away she thought vexedly that it was mean of Ilse to tell him. And tomorrow night at the Gannets' there'd be teasing hints about her 'date' and she'd feel horribly uncomfortable. But she couldn't get out of it, the Chief's invitation was a command!

She pushed all that into the back of her mind and spent the next half-hour telling Gino a wonderful story about the father he'd never seen, the father whom the Browns, with the guilt of the five hundred pounds on their conscience, had turned into a monster for a shy, bewildered little boy. Perhaps, deep in his heart, the child had known all the time that they were lying. He didn't hide under the bedclothes and shut his ears to what Sheila was saying. He listened bright-eyed, intensely absorbed, as she spoke of the tall, handsome man who had wandered up and down the world, making his lovely music, and always hoping that some day . . .

'He was looking for me,' the child interrupted her. And there was such a radiance in his small white face that she was suddenly afraid.

Victor mustn't let him down. Somehow, at no matter what cost, it must be made possible for them to be together always.

That was the prayer in her heart as she slipped into the ward just before nine o'clock that evening. She had met the Night Sister and promised her that if the child was asleep she would go away again. His bed had been moved into a corner and partially screened, and he was waiting for her, too excited to sleep. She sat down beside him and tuned in her little transistor.

The hospital by night reminded her of her father's illness: the ticking, purring quiet, as though you were suddenly made aware of the machinery that ran the place. The nurse writing at her table under the lamp, the vases of flowers ranged on the short corridor between the two sets of swing doors, like ballet dancers in the wings. Through a glass door she could see two masked figures busy in the milk-room, getting ready to give the babies their late feed. Then the world was narrowed to a little boy's bed behind the screens. His hand groped out and held hers tightly. The sounds that came from the magic box scared him. They had just caught the crazy teenage whistling and squealing before the rhythm group was faded out and Victor stood alone in the spotlight.

'Now!' whispered Sheila.

He played a wild czardas. She felt Gino's hand tremble, saw his eyes grow big with wonder and delight.

'Is that my daddy?' And then, because ordinary words failed him: 'Damnblasthell . . . damnblasthell!'

'Listen, he's playing for *you*.'

It was Schumann's 'Slumber Song', the very stuff of dreams. And then he was playing the 'Méditation', as

he had promised: the lovely notes of exaltation and
longing fell one by one into the soft hush of night, as
though he stood there, just beyond the shadows, and one
more step would bring his living presence. . . . Tears
were running down Sheila's cheeks; she had never felt
her heart so deeply stirred.

Victor had taken his theatre audience by surprise, and
in the hushed instant before the applause crashed out
Sheila switched off the set. She turned to Gino. He was
asleep, his brow smoothed out, his long lashes making
shadows on his cheeks. She tucked the bedclothes round
him and stood up. And then she saw Timothy Redfern.
He was standing in the shadows. His hands were deep
in the pockets of his white coat and she couldn't see his
face. She had been right, then. There *was* a living
presence. But not Victor's.

He didn't say a word; he fell into step beside her, held
open the ward doors. When one of the nurses came
hurrying, he motioned her back. ' It's all right. I
looked in to see Franzl. Doctor Sawley will be round
presently to attend to the transfusion. You have the
blood in the fridge? Right. I think we're getting somewhere at last.'

He caught Sheila up with long strides.

' They lock the side door after the night staff comes on.
You'll have to cross the yard to get out. This way.'

She could find her way perfectly, but when she started
to tell him so, something happened to her voice. In the
shadowy yard there were still a couple of cars parked,
and to one side there was a grotesque still life of scaffolding and buckets. After the stocktaking, the spring lick
of paint. . . . A painter had left his can in a silly place
and she stumbled over it. Red's hand shot out and
steadied her.

She felt a tremor run through his arm. He gave an
odd laugh.

' Blast that fellow and his music!'

And then he had Sheila in his arms, he was kissing her

passionately—her throat, her eyes, her lips. She willed herself to resist him; and in spite of that, with burning shame and a crazy sort of rapture, she felt her lips respond to his, her limbs go weak. He didn't know his own strength; his arm hurt her and she made a little sound.

'Forgive me,' said Red, and went on kissing her.

Then someone knocked over a bucket with a hideous tinny clamour at the other side of the yard. Sheila glimpsed a figure in a nurse's stripey dress just disappearing round the corner, and something in the waggling, bouncy walk suggested Nurse Porson. She could scarcely have failed to recognize the Registrar—his build, the tawny hair, and his white coat standing out against the dark wall. And naturally she would take the girl with him for Ilse Devon.

That thought brought her sharply back to her senses. What madness had seized them both?

Red said in a reckless, unsteady voice: 'A fine moment for someone to kick the bucket! Not that we really mind, do we?' He made to draw her towards him again. 'Kiss me!'

Sheila felt a little sick. There was a blaze of anger in her eyes.

'Don't touch me!' she said swiftly. And then her voice gave out again.

She was running from him, her world dark about her.

CHAPTER IX

'We'll run you there, of course,' Ilse said when they discussed going to Dr Gannet's for Saturday evening. And she had added teasingly: 'Can't have you wandering round the streets in a daze, Sheila dear!'

She made it so clear that she could have the Boss Man running round at her bidding, and that they would be going to the Gannets' together. Sheila was thankful now that she had shied off it, on the grounds that she needed exercise and would quite enjoy finding her own way there through the park.

She was so anxious not to be late, and she found the house so easily—a beautiful, architect-designed place with a smooth red drive and flowering trees—that she arrived much too early. Mrs Gannet was sweet about that, settled her in a comfortable armchair and chatted to her about her work at the hospital and how wonderful it was to find a ward teacher in these days. It wasn't just politeness. Sheila felt she really was interested in her husband's staff.

Sheila found herself telling her all about her father's illness and the compulsion she had felt to be near home and spend as much time as she could with her parents. That made it easy to ask if she might be excused early tonight, for the weekend was the time when she could lend a hand at home.

'But of course, my dear,' said Mrs Gannet kindly. 'Once the shop talk is over and the doctor starts showing his Swiss pictures there'll be no getting away, so I'll have coffee served early and you can slip off home whenever it suits you. I'm afraid that means Timothy and Ilse won't be able to give you a lift.'

Quite so, thought Sheila, who wanted above anything to avoid making a threesome with Red and Ilse tonight.

Mrs Gannet sighed a little and confessed: 'Those two are keeping us in suspense!' She searched Sheila's face. 'It's a tragic story to which there could still be a happy ending.'

'Ilse told me about her husband's accident,' said Sheila.

'A shocking affair. And a hard blow to Timothy. Mark Devon was his best friend. They went through medical school together and came to M.G.H. for their first house jobs. Ilse had just been put in charge of the physiotherapy.' She smiled a little. 'Timothy and

Mark had so many tastes in common. Perhaps it wasn't surprising they both fell in love with the same girl. Well, Ilse made her choice.' A moment's silence, and then Mrs Gannet said: ' Timothy was best man at their wedding, and then he cleared out and signed on as a ship's surgeon. Until that happened, I don't think any of us realized how deeply he cared.'

Now there was a longer pause. Sheila stared at her hands, tightly knotted in her lap to hide their trembling.

Mrs Gannet sighed again. ' Poor Ilse, her married life was over before Mark had really got established. And the business side of the practice was all haywire. Such a muddle!' She hesitated, as though weighing up if what she was about to say counted as a disloyalty. ' No one can say that the loss of a young, useful life is for the best. But Ilse was hardly cut out to be a family doctor's wife. Mark disappointed her when he went into practice instead of specializing. But now, of course——'

Of course.

Timothy Redfern had chucked the merchant navy when Ilse became a widow. The Children's Ward had always seemed to Sheila a queer choice for his return to hospital life, but now she understood. He was well in with the Gannets, who were personal friends of himself and Ilse. With the Chief's backing he'd be in the running for a higher appointment eventually, scarce though they were in this ' line'. What counted most, Sheila saw, was that an opening had occurred just at the right moment in the hospital where Ilse was working. At that, it was a job which would bring them constantly in touch. Did you need to look any further for his motive?

She had no doubt at all that Ilse, the ambitious, would some day be a consultant's wife, after all.

Only one thing didn't make sense. That little scene in the hospital yard last night. She had been kissed before —but never like that; never with passion and hunger and glory.

Was it just the spell of Victor Cort's music which had been flung over them both and held them in a net, there among the deep-etched shadows? Her heart cried out: No, no. He kissed me as if he loved me. *Me, and me only.* Every instinct in her proclaimed that this was the truth. But reason—and Mrs Gannet—said otherwise.

When he took her in his arms he was just yielding to a moment's folly, betraying Ilse's trust. Ilse had broken his heart once, when she passed him by and chose his friend. But he still loved her, still hoped. He had given up the sea, which had drawn him since he was a boy, in order to be near her. She forced herself to remember that.

Mrs Gannet's friendly, charming voice talked on and on. But when Sheila raised her eyes, dark and tortured by the inner conflict, the flow of words was suddenly checked. Mrs Gannet looked at her guest in dismay, wondering what she could have said to hurt her feelings.

With relief she heard Timothy Redfern's Jaguar stop outside the house.

'They're here! And I hope Hamish Dee and his wife will be looking in later to see our Swiss transparencies. My husband is just giving them a tinkle now. I do so love a party, you know! I hope you'll feel quite at home, dear, and really enjoy yourself. When we meet socially, there's none of that silly red tape between a consultant and his staff!'

Was she trying to give reassurance, guessing that Sheila was in a panic at the idea of chatting to the great Alexander Gannet over coffee? The idea almost made Sheila smile. The Chief was a pet and had been her staunch friend right from the start, when he was defending her job against the meanness of Mr Porson and Mr Mercks. It was Red and Ilse she dreaded meeting now.

Her nerves were stretched taut. What would she see in Red's eyes when he looked at her? Would it be shame, embarrassment, an urgent plea not to give him away? Or would his eyes go on saying what he had whispered last night. *Kiss me!* Her whole being had leapt to him like a flame. She trembled now, remembering.

After all, the Chief kept him talking in the hall and Ilse appeared alone. Mrs Gannet kissed her affectionately and said how charming she looked in her cocktail dress. It was like a brief, glittering tunic of chain mail; above it her pallor seemed to glow out, her dark hair to shine like a starling's wing. Sheila thought she looked wonderful. The whole effect of a poised, confident woman who knew exactly where she was going, made her feel young and awkward, her little nylon two-piece in delphinium blue somehow too simple, home-made. As the thought crossed her mind she felt ashamed. Her mother's dressmaking was neat and painstaking, even if the result somehow just failed to have style.

Since James Thorne's illness the sewing machine had been busy and there were pins everywhere. She was doing her bit to help the family income. And she had put urgent work aside to finish Sheila's two-piece so that she could wear it at the Gannets' coffee evening. If only Ilse's eyes weren't so critical behind the friendly smile!

She was asking how Gino had reacted to hearing his father on the radio. Before Sheila could answer, the Chief and his Registrar came in. They were discussing the little Austrian boy, who had been put on a plane that morning for home. They were talking about his mysterious case-notes—like crossword clues, Dr Gannet said. He tilted his head back to smile up at his tall assistant.

'You coped splendidly. I'm afraid the boy gave you some bad moments.'

Certainly Red was looking haggard, immensely tired and under a strain. He didn't directly face Sheila, just stood there chatting to the Gannets, but she knew he was intensely aware of her, as she was of him. She felt a guilty, tingling gladness in his presence; suddenly she was more alive. And when his eyes for a brief instant locked with hers, the colour rushed into her cheeks and she felt an inner commotion that made nonsense of what they were saying; voices, words, became just a confused murmur like leaves in the wind or the tide on a seashore. For his eyes possessed her, as his lips had possessed her, made her his. *It wasn't just a mad impulse, it wasn't just the music. He has never kissed Ilse like that. He loves me, he loves me!*

Suddenly everyone was looking at her, and for a ghastly moment she thought she had shouted the words aloud. But it was simply that Dr Gannet, seating them all with one commanding wave of the hand, had begun talking about the ward. He was full of new notions he had brought back from the congress and tossed off brilliant schemes—some practical, some scatty—like a display of fireworks, leaving Sheila breathless with wonder. Red—away from the formality of the hospital—doused some of them promptly; other ideas they hammered into something useful, calling now for Ilse's opinion, now Sheila's. Dr Gannet had a briefcase crammed with brochures, large glossy photographs, hasty jottings of his own. All sorts of gadgets to enable the bedfast child to take part in lessons and games. A device for turning the pages of a book without hands, a new type of cot which made postural drainage easier when a child couldn't simply hang over the side and 'cough it up', as Sheila found them doing like a barnyard chorus each morning.

The pictures were sent round, and when Red passed her one his fingers crushed hers for a moment with an ardent, secret pressure that frightened and thrilled her.

'I foresaw one snag when we engaged a ward teacher,' Dr Gannet remarked. 'Dovetailing your work with Ilse's, if you didn't happen to hit it off.'

'But we do,' Ilse said instantly. 'We get along like a house afire!' For the first time Sheila couldn't meet her eyes. She was thankful the orthopaedic surgeon and his wife arrived just then. The business session was over. Dr Gannet bustled round getting ready his projector and screen and his wife slipped away to make coffee. Hamish Dee came across and put in a nice word about Sheila's work with young Stephen. 'It'll be a feather in our cap if we get the boy through his exams from a hospital bed!'

Sheila scarcely knew what she answered. She had just seen Ilse dip into Timothy Redfern's jacket pocket, bring out her little enamelled vanity case and touch up her lipstick. If she had flourished a diamond engagement ring before their eyes it wouldn't have spoken more clearly of their relationship. That one confident, casual gesture brought Sheila up with a jerk. These two belonged together and always had done. Would Red have left his ship and taken this unlikely post at M.G.H. if he didn't mean to marry Ilse? Would Ilse have presumed on a slight friendship to act as she did when they were together, in company? No, no, no. She must have been out of her mind to imagine Red's kisses meant a thing. He had forgotten the incident already, and so must she. Quickly. But *quickly*.

She nibbled a sandwich, sipped coffee, smiled dutifully at Mr Dee's jokes. Something about a plaster of paris birthday cake concocted for an unpopular member of staff in his own student days. 'Beautifully iced it was, too.' Dr Gannet trotted out his tale of the haggis sent up to the lab for the pathologist's report. He turned to the Registrar. 'Now then, Redfern, we expect you to cap that with something bloodcurdling from the ship's galley.' He glanced at Hamish Dee. 'This fellow yarns away to the kids about ships and sailing, but never a word can I get out of him about his adventures in the sick-bay.'

The young doctor's face wore a strange expression, bitter and bleak. Sheila felt a stab of compassion. Going to sea hadn't been the fulfilment of Red's boyhood dream, merely exile from the woman he loved. She felt sure of that now, and the knowledge lay heavy on her heart. She snatched thankfully at the first chance to murmur her excuses and slip away when the coffee things were being cleared.

Red followed her out to the hall with long strides.

'You're not leaving so early? Before the Chief does his stuff?'

'I'm sorry. I'll see the slides another time, perhaps. You see, I—I promised to be home early.'

'I'll give you a lift.'

But Ilse was suddenly there, too. It was a humiliation for Sheila that they were making a drama of it, when she'd hoped to slip off with no fuss at all.

'Red, I'm surprised at you!' said Ilse, one hand resting lightly on his arm, her delicate brows raised in a mischievous smile. 'You can't have forgotten Sheila's Saturday date!'

Exit line, thought Sheila bitterly. Mrs Gannet waved to her from the top of the steps; Ilse and Red were grouped behind her. And as Sheila hurried off into the darkness she took with her the memory of his angry, bewildered look. Why should he resent her having a date? What business was it of his, anyway? His voice seemed to follow her mockingly: *Kiss me! Kiss me*. . . . The hot tears blinded her. She walked stumblingly, her breath coming very fast, as if she had been running. On and on in the darkness. When she reached home she had put a foolish dream out of her heart for ever.

* * *

On Monday morning Gino was giving trouble. 'Such language!' said Sister Bain, her lips tight. 'All this hullabaloo because he's to go down for a cardiograph this morning.'

Sheila felt sickeningly disappointed. What had she expected all of a sudden? A plaster angel, as unreal as the birthday cake Mr Dee had joked about?

'The cardiograph is nothing to worry about,' Sister said very briskly. 'It's just Red being fussy. He always expects complications and acts accordingly.

He'd be awful with children of his own, so perhaps it's as well——' She stopped short, then returned to her grievance. 'Of course, if people will come upsetting that child. Late nights and everything.'

'I'm sorry, Sister. I hoped so much from it.'

Sister looked uncomfortable. She said rapidly: 'We're hoping the Browns will take him home just as soon as the doctor permits. That's partly why he asked for a radiograph. To be on the safe side before we let the child go.' She hesitated. 'But they're going to have a job with him this morning, the way he's taking on! He might behave for you. If you could possibly find time, round about coffee break?'

Sheila found Gino stormy-eyed and sullen.

'So you're going to be wired up like a space man, Gino! Now this is something I must see. You don't mind if I come along?'

A hot small hand slid into hers and held on very tight.

'While we're down there my daddy might come for me. He's going to come *soon*. And if he doesn't see me here he'll think I've gone with Mrs Brown. He won't know where to look for me——'

'We'll leave word with Staff, shall we?'

'He came before and didn't find me. Doctor Red sent him away.'

'It was a mistake. I promise you that when he comes again, he won't leave without seeing you.'

A radiance came into his face. He trusted her completely. And she felt close to heartbreak. The weight of that five hundred pounds on their conscience might compel the Browns to take him back; they might even arrange with Victor Cort that he saw the boy sometimes. But it didn't add up to a little boy's dream for tomorrow!

They went across to the cardiac unit—Gino wrapped in blankets in a wheelchair, Nurse Velta and Sheila walking beside him. Two pretty technicians took over. They moved Gino to a couch, then suddenly they were called away and a maddening wait began. Nurse Velta was fidgety, her mind on the ward chores. Eventually Sheila sent her off to get instructions. She was back in a couple of minutes, and Timothy Redfern was with her. He looked very put out.

'I'm sorry about this. One of the physicians suddenly wanted a heart investigation done on the ward. The case must be critical, but all the same, it's abominable to keep you waiting around like this. Escort duty isn't part of your job, and Sister knows it. And with the child so upset——'

Then he blinked a little. Gino, snuggling into his blankets, looked drowsy and happy. He was holding Sheila's hand tightly.

'I offered,' said Sheila. 'It was coffee break anyway, and I left the children plenty to do.'

His eyes burned intensely blue. He stared at her for a long moment and then shrugged. Without another word he turned away. He must have stirred things up to some purpose, for in no time at all the technicians were back. It was all quite commonplace to them, but Sheila found it a scarey business, in spite of the build-up about spacemen. They smeared jelly on the skin before attaching the wires to the child's arms and legs. The apparatus was switched on with a hum and a buzz—and she marvelled that the little boy wasn't afraid. As long as she was there with him, he could take anything. Behind his head an automatic pen recorded the heart's action on squared paper which came out like ticker tape. It was all over in a few minutes. As Nurse Velta got ready to take Gino back to the ward, Sheila lingered a moment, staring at the squiggles on the paper.

'Is it good or bad?'

She should have known better than to ask. The senior technician gave her a snooty look and said: 'The recording will be sent up to Dr Redfern as quickly as possible.'

They were so cagey about clinical details! Sister Bain might drop a hint, or she might be close as an oyster. She daren't ask the Registrar. That made Dick Sawley her best bet, and when he was on the ward that afternoon she asked him point-blank if the rheumatic infection had damaged Gino's heart, or was the cardiograph just routine when the patient got to the convalescent stage.

'We've a few cases due for convalescence at Scadcroft,' Dick Sawley replied, not answering her question at all. 'Old Red likes to get the asthma children out there for country air as early as possible—once we've excluded fur, feathers and pollen as the cause of the trouble—and there's this laddie with a bronchiectasis, blowing bubbles through a leaky lung: he'll do well out there. And when she's finished her course of injections Norina is due for the big push, too.'

But not a word about Gino. The omission was so pointed, it filled Sheila with alarm. She saw the little boy listening intently to the radio, which he had ignored till now. He was hoping to hear the magic fiddle again. Or his eyes would go to the ward doors with such expectancy that she could hardly bear to see it. Sister Bain and the doctors so obviously took it for granted that they would see nothing more of Victor Cort. He had flashed across the sky of Marbury like a meteor with a tail of fire; the fire of his music. Perhaps it would be another eight years . . . She could even see that in Sister Bain's eyes, and in Timothy Redfern's too, she had done something cruel and wrong by raising the child's hopes. Then she remembered his courage this morning and knew she had done right.

The busy week slipped by. There was no news from Victor Cort, nothing from the Browns; not a word about that cardiograph, either. She could almost imagine she had dreamt the whole thing. Then on Friday Sister Bain asked if she would like to see Scadcroft.

'The ambulance will be leaving at half-past four. We have three little ones and Norina going. Usually the children look on it as a great treat, but Norina isn't keen.

I doubt if she's spent a day in the country in her whole life! If you could put it over to her as an adventure——' Then she gave Sheila one of her funny looks. 'It's after school hours, but I don't want our Registrar to think we're pushing escort duty on to you!'

So he had complained about her being sent with Gino!

'I'd love to see Scadcroft,' she said firmly.

She bought a little sketch-pad for Norina.

'There'll be all sorts of flowers you can paint, birds we never coax to our bird-tray, the woods and fields. Suppose you send me the sketches you do, and I'll pin them up for the children here to enjoy?'

She had said just the right thing. Norina was suddenly impatient to be out in the country, sketching from morning till night. Besides the children, there were two adult patients in the ambulance. 'A kettle of red herrings,' Nurse Connell called it. She sat with a baby on her knee, while Sheila kept the other children in order and tried to glimpse the countryside through the dark glass of the ambulance windows. Then they were driving through big gates and up a winding gravel road between lawns and shrubberies, with huts dotted among the greenery. Only the children's block looked in the least like a hospital. There were open-sided wards and balconies; and while Nurse Connell and the babies were whisked off by an Irish friend of hers who happened to be on reception, Sheila went to see Norina's cubicle.

The older children had these separate rooms, two tiers of them opening off galleries, like a section of honeycomb. Norina looked round the stark white box of a room and said: 'I want to write on the wall.'

'Wouldn't it be more fun to cut a stencil and paint a flower frieze? I could come over some evening and help you to get started.'

Norina gave her an imploring look. 'I'd rather come back with you now, miss. I don't like it here.'

'Give it a chance! Look, when you unpack after tea and put up your photographs, it will make all the difference in the world. And I can see some girls strolling in the garden, you'll soon make friends. I'm sure they dig Elvis and Adam! There may even be a record-player.'

'Super,' said Norina in a stony voice. She sat on the edge of the bed, a plain, overgrown girl with untidy hair and a head full of romantic dreams that she couldn't put into words.

But she *could* put them into glorious daubs of colour, Sheila knew. As Matron showed her round the place before giving her a cup of tea in her quarters, she plugged away valiantly at the idea of a flower frieze for that bare, hygienic cubicle.

'I could get her some powder to mix herself. It's a glorious feeling, mixing your own paints.'

'But messy,' said Matron.

'Ye . . . es. She could spread newspapers. And if she did splash at all, a little turps——' She stopped dead.

Matron had pushed open a door which stood ajar. And there, in her pleasant chintzy sitting-room, was Dr Redfern, drinking tea and smiling in an infuriating way.

'Don't say you haven't been warned, Matron! Miss Thorne has turned the Children's Ward upside down, and now she means to start on Scadcroft!'

Matron said in a sprightly tone: 'Oh, I knew what to expect! Mrs Devon told me about the bird-tray: how delighted Sister Bain was with the children's clean plates till the nurses who were making beds found all the crusts and crumbs hoarded under the pillows!'

Sheila went crimson. She hadn't known Ilse Devon came out to Scadcroft. Was she here today? Was that why Red had driven out? But no, from his conversation with Matron over the cup of tea it was clear he had come to look at a case the Chief was worried about. They got that settled, he put his cup down and said briskly: 'Well, Miss Thorne, if you're ready——'

He had timed it beautifully, for at that same moment Sheila saw the ambulance pass the window. Nurse

Connell was sitting beside the driver and chattering fifty to the dozen. It was perfectly obvious Red was set on driving Sheila back to town. Well, it would be an opportunity to ask him about Gino's cardiograph. If only she were not certain, deep down, that he had made the opportunity for different reasons.

She looked fixedly ahead of her as they drove through the gates, and once he had negotiated the tricky corner and was on a straight stretch of road she asked in a little rush: 'There's something I must ask you. About Gino. That recording.'

Timothy Redfern growled: 'You don't think I've wangled this in order to talk shop?'

'It's very important. I—I wish you'd tell me the truth. Is Gino going to be fit and well or . . . or an invalid?'

For some moments he didn't speak. He seemed to be giving all his attention to the road ahead. When he spoke it was in a harsh, jerky voice.

'We've done all we could. I'm satisfied the nursing care has been excellent. But the damage is there. The heart "compensates", of course; and various things can be done for him when he reaches the teens.' Then, his face suddenly convulsed: 'God, I swore it shouldn't happen. This is what makes me see red: a child's disability and suffering, while one stands helpless——'

A heavy lorry appeared from nowhere, holding the white line. The Jaguar had to swerve. Straightening out again, Red said: 'For a long time ahead that child is going to need care. And any idea you might have that he's fit to knock about the world with that father of his . . . It's no go. Do you understand? If he tries to get possession of Gino I shall do everything I can to prevent it.'

Sheila couldn't speak; her throat ached with pity and grief.

The Jaguar had slowed down. Timothy Redfern was looking at her, his eyes intensely blue.

'And another thing. Don't take your cases so desperately to heart! Norina will soon settle down at Scadcroft. Stephen has a first-class brain and will get somewhere in the world, even if he doesn't pass examinations from a hospital bed. As for Gino, he'll learn to live within the limitations of a leaky heart-valve till they decide he's the right age for the surgeon to weigh up the risks, if he's really handicapped. Meanwhile the almoner will sort things out for him. It isn't your job or mine.' He paused. 'Which brings me to the thing I want to get straight with you. It isn't easy to find the words.'

Sheila tensed up. She would have given anything to avoid this moment. He was going to apologize for what had happened last Friday night, and every word he spoke would make her humiliation deeper.

She said in a strangled whisper: 'Don't. Please don't say it.'

'But I must. Ilse joked about your "Saturday date" and you didn't just laugh it off, it upset you. There *is* somebody, isn't there? You can't be serious about Dick Sawley. I have an idea you're meeting this Cort fellow, that he's working on your sympathy, getting at you through the boy.'

Sheila went quite white. It was so utterly unexpected, so far from what she had imagined he was going to say to her. She gasped out: 'That's unpardonable!'

'But is it true?' Red demanded relentlessly. 'There are reasons why I must know the truth.'

Hands clenched, eyes blazing, Sheila half turned to face him.

'And there are reasons why it's none of your business, Doctor Redfern.'

That he should dare to question her about her friends, when he and Ilse . . . Oh, he was contemptible! And she had thought him a man of strict honour! Suddenly his left hand was on hers, he looked into her quivering, averted face.

'I want the truth. What is Victor Cort to you?'

She snatched her hands free, and said wildly: 'He's nothing to me. I think I hate men. *All* men. Will you please drive me home?'

Her mother came running out as the Jaguar drew up at the gate. Red must have heard her as she called out, excited and in a fluster:

'Who do you think we've got here? Victor Cort! And he's been waiting for you an hour!'

CHAPTER X

That tears it, Sheila thought dully.

Red must think her false and deceitful, and she had found him out, too! For Ilse Devon's sake he had given up the sea and they were as good as engaged; but that didn't rule out making love to another girl and acting as if he had a right to choose her friends. And this was the man for whom the nurses scuttled round, keeping things shipshape and Bristol fashion, afraid of his frown, preening themselves if they won a grudging word of praise; this was the Red Admiral of whom Miss Furlong stood in awe, the man Dick Sawley and young Stephen made their hero. She knew a different Timothy Redfern, unworthy of this high regard.

But it was bitter that he should drive off now, his foot down viciously on the accelerator, a scowl on his brow, believing she had lied to him about Victor Cort. With a hot and bursting heart she followed her mother into the house.

'Mr Cort has been to the hospital and someone there let him have your address. He's been telling us about the little boy. When you mentioned the child's name to us it rang a bell. Because, of course, we'd met Mr Cort on the television screen. . . . His wonderful, wonderful playing! And I can hardly believe he's here in our little house, just sitting there like an ordinary person, having a cup of tea with James. He's charming, Sheila dear, really charming.'

Victor had exerted himself, Sheila perceived, and made a conquest. How different from her first meeting with him in the little café near the theatre! He came towards her now, smiling, took her hand and held it a moment, bowing over it with Latin grace—the years of wandering about the world hadn't been for nothing—and said he was so grateful for her kindness to the *bambino*, he simply had to come along and thank her in person.

'You'll have a meal with us, Mr Cort?' Mary Thorne insisted, her face glowing. 'I'm afraid it will be very simple, a casserole dish—it's almost ready. You see, we wait till Sheila is home and have it all together.'

He declined gracefully. The show must go on. In exactly five minutes he had to leave and catch his Sheffield train, or else . . . He rolled up his eyes expressively.

'Oh, we wouldn't want you to be late for the theatre! Your public——' She was in a flutter of distress. 'But at least a sandwich?'

There wasn't even time for a sandwich. 'But don't let me keep you from your preparations, Mrs Thorne.'

'So thoughtful!' whispered Sheila's mother, as she satisfied herself there was still tea in the pot and then bustled off to the kitchen, taking James with her to 'lend a hand', so that Sheila and their V.I.P. were left together.

Sheila began to apologize for being so late home, but he brushed that aside. Abandoning the part of gracious guest, he dropped into a chair, rubbing an irritable hand over his face, which sagged with strain and fatigue. He looked terrible.

'How long is it since you ate anything?' demanded Sheila, really alarmed. 'You can't rush back to Sheffield and give a performance when you're in this state!'

Victor laughed harshly. 'Do you think my public

would notice the difference? If I played the fiddle standing on my head, that might *send* them!'

His famous gesture of saluting with an invisible fiddle bow held such weary disillusionment that Sheila felt more worried still. She was at a loss what to say, and brought out lamely: 'Are you getting good houses?'

'Packed. Just the same, we close tomorrow. Two miserable weeks instead of the long run we expected. The theatre lease has run out. The place is to be pulled down to make room for a supermarket, and the demolition squad is practically squatting at the stage door.'

'Oh, no!' She really felt sick with distress. 'What an awful thing to happen! But there'll be other bookings for the company, surely?'

'We're splitting up. I'm going out on my own. Television, records, a solo spot in cabaret, maybe. There is a tide . . . and I have a hunch this is mine.'

Sheila couldn't speak. It sounded so chancy, so precarious; and just when she was hoping and praying he could build a secure future for Gino.

'Oh, to hell with the theatre!' He stood up, making a violent movement with his arms as if to brush all these concerns away like crumbs from a tablecloth. He began pacing agitatedly up and down, and over his shoulder he flung at her: 'I've been to the hospital. I've seen my son.' He turned round again, and this time there was no fake, no pose. His eyes shone with tears and his whole face was working. He was in the grip of a tremendous emotion. '*My son*. He's so like Giovanna, it turned my heart over. So little and frail.'

'I know,' whispered Sheila, her own eyes stinging.

Victor mastered himself and said in a flat, controlled voice:

'They didn't leave me alone with him. The Sister was there all the time, and afterwards she had the doctor lined up, this red-headed cock o' the roost, in case I had questions. You can bet I had questions. And he didn't wrap up the answers, I got the brutal truth.'

Now he stared in front of him, reciting the words like a lesson.

'The rheumatic infection has burnt itself out, the child no longer has pain or fever. But he isn't out of the wood. His heart is damaged. He explained that to me. In the course of the disease, when the child has aching joints and feels ill, the same process is injuring the valves of the heart; but the symptoms don't come on till later, so he has to be kept in bed even if he feels all right. After a while he'll be moved to some convalescent place.'

'Scadcroft.'

'That's right. And meanwhile, if I make any attempt to take my boy away against medical advice, he personally will see that action is taken in the interests of the child.' A bitter laugh. 'Who is he to decide what's in the interests of the child? He made it plain that the big idea is to keep Gino away from me.'

Sheila gripped the table. Every bit of colour was drained from her face, only her eyes were blazing. She was so *angry*. Red had come to Scadcroft straight from the interview. This was his reason for needing to know exactly what Victor Cort meant to her. He wanted to be sure of his ground before he went ahead with his threats and his bullying. Well, she'd been warned! 'Talk about throwing his weight around,' Sister Bain had confided, before she had even met the man. Victor Cort, with his stormy temperament, his artistic feeling, his restless, Bohemian way of life, stood for everything he hated. Discipline, rules and regulations, the top brass piped aboard with due ceremony—that was Red's scheme of things.

Victor dropped into a chair, his head between his hands. He said brokenly: 'I've lost him.'

'Oh, please, don't feel like that about it.'

'What have they told him? He's scared of me. I tried to make friends—with Sister standing by—but he hid under the clothes and I couldn't get a word out of him.'

'I expect he was just disappointed because you didn't stroll in playing the fiddle,' said Sheila with a faint smile. 'He's been watching for you every day since he heard you over the air. Oh, if you'd seen him then! He was so proud of you.'

Victor groaned. 'Proud of me! It's my own fault that we're strangers to one another. But I swear I thought I was acting for the best when I let the Browns have him.' He sprang up again, consumed with restlessness. 'That's all going to be changed. I'll win Gino over. I'll give him everything in the world. He isn't going to any hole in the country—I'll look after him. Just let them try and keep him from me——'

Already he'd forgotten that the closing of the theatre was a serious calamity. He was impatient for the Sheffield run to be over, the twice-nightly appearances were just a bind, keeping him from bigger opportunities. Another television spot, perhaps a contract; gramophone records.

'That's where the money is. My first L.P. will be a smash hit, just you wait!' He laughed, the black mood falling from him. '"The Fun and Laughter Show" may be all washed up, but I'm just starting. The world's my oyster and my fiddle-bow is the sword that will open it.' He made his lordly flourish with the invisible bow. 'London, here I come!'

'Shall you go straight from the theatre tomorrow night?'

He frowned. Practical details irritated him. 'No, I'm holing up for the weekend with Lena and Frank.'

As she looked puzzled, he snapped his fingers impatiently.

'I must have mentioned them. Frank Tatlow plays clarinet in the orchestra at the variety theatre and he and his wife put me up during the run of the show here. They're fine people, I want you to meet them. . . . Yes, of course. You must come along on Sunday. Just drop in any time to suit yourself.'

He began scribbling directions on an old envelope.

'I can't possibly barge in on complete strangers like that!' Sheila objected. 'And in any case——'

She was too deeply involved already in this thing. Hadn't she been warned again and again not to interfere in the private lives of patients? The future of one little boy concerned her passionately, but she had made things more difficult for him by bringing his father into the picture.

Perhaps Victor read her thought. The buoyancy went out of him suddenly. The eyes that were exactly like Gino's eyes gave her a reproachful look and he said humbly: 'Forgive me. I take too much for granted. But I beg you to come to Frank and Lena's on Sunday and we'll see if we can't work out something for Gino between us.' He paused a moment. 'The Browns let me down. That's clear from the enquiries I've made. Gino can't go back to them. But I have three good friends I'd trust to the ends of the earth: Frank and Lena—and you.' Before she could prevent him, he had taken her hands and kissed them. She snatched them free as her mother bustled in with sandwiches and cake on a tray. It was so beautifully arranged—there was a pretty lace doiley under the cake and the sandwiches were delicate triangles with all the crusts cut off—that Sheila felt shamed when Victor still refused to have anything.

'Dear lady, forgive me,' he begged, with the smile that would make a woman forgive him anything. 'There's only just time to catch my train. And, good lord, I've a taxi ticking away somewhere.' His departure was like a wind that sets all the leaves whirling. From the pavement he waved and called: 'Sunday. I'm counting on you.'

As they went back indoors Sheila explained reluctantly: 'He wants me to meet some friends of his. Musicians.'

'But how kind!' cried Mrs Thorne. 'Success hasn't spoilt him in the least. We were so afraid you'd find it dull living at home, Sheila, my dear. But last weekend there was Doctor Gannet's party and now you're asked to a musical evening! You'll take your guitar, of course? One never knows where such an invitation may lead. We shall see you on telly yet!'

It was cruel to undeceive her, Sheila thought wryly. She had the whimsical notion that her mother's imagination performed the Indian rope trick on the slightest provocation: threw up a ladder, hooked it on to nothingness and had her daughter climbing nimbly towards the stars!

But James Thorne thought in facts and called a spade a spade, as any inveterate gardener should. At the moment he said nothing, but his silence on the subject of Victor Cort was eloquent enough. Sheila and her mother discovered him polishing off the sandwiches, and his silence held not only resentment at being kept waiting all this while for his evening meal, but a practical man's distrust of temperamental musicians.

He needn't worry, thought Sheila. And that went for Dr Timothy Redfern, too. He had more than half a notion she was in love with Victor. The truth of the matter was something so different! If she went to the Tatlows' on Sunday evening it would be solely for Gino's sake. She was clinging to the hope that these good friends of Victor's would offer the child a secure, comfortable home, love him, watch over his delicate health. The more she thought about it, the more she liked it as a solution of the problem that was endlessly in her mind.

But as soon as she saw the house she knew the thing wouldn't work.

It was a tall, gaunt house in a row behind shabby wrought-iron gates. The terrace had once been fashionable and was now sadly fallen from gentility to become offices and agencies and cheap commercial schools. There was a brass plate on the door of the end house, setting out Lena Tatlow's qualifications as a teacher of music. There were dark green rep curtains, giving the windows a forbidding darkness. The hall was dark and echoing, too, and in the big front room there seemed to be nothing but a grand piano and stacks of music which overflowed from the piano top on to the chairs and the floor. The carpet was threadbare, the Steinway glorious —and that conveyed to Sheila, at the very first glance round, precisely the scale of values in a dedicated musician's life. If the picture needed a final touch, it was provided by the closed coke stove, with ash scattered on the hearth before it and a coffee pot and plate of cinnamon toast sitting on top; used cups scattered around, like accidentals on a sheet of music.

Victor's introduction was of the simplest. 'Lena, Frank. This is Sheila Thorne from the hospital.'

Sheila saw a slightly built man with short-sighted eyes and a vague smile of great sweetness. He was fitting a new reed to his clarinet and practising little soft runs up and down the instrument to try it out. Lena was a dark-haired woman, skinny, sallow and vital. She was copying music with exquisite precision and looked up briefly.

'Lovely to meet you. Can you hold out on coffee and toast while I'm finishing this?' She dipped her fine pen into a little bottle of Indian ink and went on with the work. To eke out the piano lessons she arranged and copied music, and most weekends Frank played with a dance-band. They were a talented, hard-working couple and Sheila liked them. But she knew already that an invalid child would never fit into the scheme of things.

In their company Victor shed his grand manner. While he discussed the cello part Lena was writing into a piece of music he was collecting up the dirty cups on an old tray and carried them off to the kitchen. Perhaps Sheila's thoughts were showing. Lena fixed her with a brilliant dark glance, prepared to be hostile and then, as it were, changed tempo in the middle of a bar.

'You can see we're Bohemians,' she said dryly. 'We wash up before a meal instead of after. I recommend it.'

Then she bent to her copying again and Frank, soft-voiced and diffident, began asking about the music Sheila did with her children at the hospital, and that quite naturally led to Gino.

Victor was still on his kitchen chores. There would never be a better moment. Sheila told them about the child's illness, keeping clinical details to the minimum and touching cautiously on his unhappy experience with the Browns. And then she found herself confiding just how precarious the child's future was, how urgent his need for love in happy home surroundings. Lena and Frank exchanged a glance.

'We're hoping that will settle itself,' said Lena, carefully wiping her pen on a handkerchief. Sheila's eyes betrayed her again. Lena explained with perfect simplicity. 'The nib will be ruined if I get any hairs on it. Blotting paper is tricky. A good smooth hankie is quite the best thing.'

'Oh, yes, I'm sure,' Sheila said, blushing.

Critically examining the nib before she put her pen away in a beat-up little leather case, Lena remarked: 'Victor needs exactly the same thing. A home, love, comfort. He's had it pretty rough all these years, poor lad, wandering up and down the world.' She crouched in an ungainly attitude, all arms and legs like a daddy-long-legs, to rake out the stove, revealing the glowing heart before she hooked the doors shut again and spoke over her shoulder. 'The thing is to have roots somewhere, then even if he wanders he'll always come back. But perhaps you're a traveller, too?'

'The furthest I've been was Paris with a school party.' She had accompanied a friend who taught in the senior school. It had been arduous and wonderful. 'Herding the children into the coach, once they'd been let loose, was like getting toothpaste back into the tube! One lad who'll be a fine electrician some day, if he doesn't get himself frizzled up before then, gave us the fright of our lives by causing the hotel lift to stick midway between floors. Another dropped a valuable camera into the lake at Versailles.'

And there had been precious moments, with the children washed off their hands, like ink and chalk at the end of a school day. A moment for slipping back to the Louvre and having another gaze at the surprisingly small and dark Mona Lisa. A moment for shopping and strolling. A whole evening at the Opéra: the crowds, the evening gowns, the great orchestra tuning up, the embarrassment because they hadn't known the *ouvreuse* expected a tip, then the whole world forgotten in the glory of *Thaïs*. Victor might also have guessed when he played the ' Méditation ' for her over the radio. . . .

She tried to recall all this for Lena and Frank, and they listened absorbed, enjoying the animation of the girl's face, her little gestures, living it with her.

But there were things she couldn't put into words. The shimmer of sunlight through the exquisite spring tracery of the trees on the boulevards. Yes, that was pure Monet. *The principal person in a picture is the light*. And an old woman hawking lilies of the valley between the little iron tables of a *café terrasse* in the dusk, her basket spilling over with their purity and fragrance. For it had been the first day of May, when lovers greeted one another with these flowers. Sheila had shaken her head and laughed and said she had no boy-friend, so what was the use?

Suddenly now it caught her breath to realize that what had been a never-to-be-forgotten adventure in her life was something woven into the everyday warp and weft of Victor Cort's roaming.

' You know, he's been everywhere,' Lena was saying. ' Rome, Athens, Istanbul, America.'

Into her fine eyes came a little girl's wistfulness. She glanced at her husband.

' Frank and I had a near miss last year. There was an idea that the dance-band would fly out to take part in a contest in Rome. Even if you don't carry off an award, it builds up a reputation! Frank doubles clarinet and tenor sax for them, you know, and I do their arrangements. The variety theatre was closed for the summer and it was our great chance. We saved up madly. At the very last minute the thing was called off, and of course we couldn't afford to go it alone. The dream of a lifetime gone for a burton!'

She met her husband's eyes and they exchanged a special sort of smile.

'Not,' said Lena, her voice very brisk, 'that we could really spare the time. Frank got some clarinet pupils at a couple of schools. Summer courses.'

Frank said gently: 'They all want to play like Mr Acker Bilk. You know: a very soft reed and just enough breath to make it vibrate. If it were any softer he wouldn't be playing at all. Clever. Very clever.'

'About Victor,' Lena said. 'Two minutes on telly can really get you somewhere. Amazing, isn't it? The recording companies are interested, and if he could only make a hit with a disc——' She threw out her hands, gave Sheila her keen, brilliant smile. 'We're trying to put over the idea that he has prospects. Naturally you have to consider all that.'

Sheila plucked up all her courage. 'I wouldn't want you to get the wrong idea. I'm here only because I'm so sure Gino could make friends with his father through his music and I believe you can help.'

'Oh!' It was a little wry exclamation of regret. 'We did so hope——'

Sheila hurried on very fast, skating over the dangerous moment:

'If it were possible—I know it's a big thing to ask —but what I had in mind was a little entertainment on the ward. Not a concert. Just something quite informal. . . . You must please tell me straight out if it's impossible.'

Lena smiled again. 'If it's really for Gino's sake, how can we refuse? We'll work out something.' Her face brightened. 'Really it could be rather fun. What do you say, Frank? There's such charming music for children. Debussy, Prokofiev——'

Frank chuckled. 'Aim high, by all means. But you know very well I'll never get by without "Stranger on the Shore" and "This can't be Love"!'

Victor appeared in the doorway. He began apologizing to Sheila for being out of the room such a long time. 'The blasted sink was full of burnt pans,' he explained.

This slight on her housekeeping left Lena Tatlow absolutely unmoved. She said enthusiastically: 'We didn't even miss you. We've been getting on like a house afire. Look, it's all fixed that we're to entertain Sheila's wardful of children when you get back from your London trip. It's for Gino's sake, but we'll give pleasure to the others at the same time. What do you say to "Peter and the Wolf" if I arrange it for the trio—piano, violin, clarinet? I'm going to plunge for Debussy—"Golliwog's Cakewalk"—as my solo. Frank hasn't much choice really. He knows already what they'll ask for! How about your party piece, that gipsy lullaby?'

Victor, hands in pockets, was scowling.

'Whose idea was this, anyway?'

'Mine,' Sheila said timidly.

Lena came to her rescue. 'I wish I'd thought of it first. I owe Marbury General a thank-you.' She swivelled to Sheila. 'In the icy weather I had a nasty fall on our front steps. Chipped a piece off my elbow—and you know how serious that is for a pianist. There's just a little stiffness. I was trekking across to the physiotherapy department for weeks and weeks and they really put me through it. The woman in charge is first-rate. Do you know her? We must certainly ask Mrs Devon to the concert.'

Sheila's heart dropped sickeningly. But Victor was making a sweeping gesture.

'Ask 'em all. I shall be playing for Gino alone.'

Frank had picked up his clarinet again and was blowing

softly through the new reed. Victor began rubbing resin on his fiddle bow.

'What happened to your arrangement of the lullaby, Lena?' he asked.

'I'll dig it out.' On her knees, she rooted through a pile of music manuscript. She called out: 'Sheila, do help yourself to coffee and toast, if it hasn't gone cold. We'll have a grand fry-up presently. Ah, here it is!'

They were round the piano, counting bars, arguing who came in where, marking repeats that were not clear in the manuscript. Frank switched on the standard lamp, and the rest of the room was plunged into a kindly and concealing dusk. Sheila crept across, rejected the toast which had gone leathery—quite the most unappetizing plate of toast she had ever seen in her life! But the coffee was hot, bitter, reviving. She could see no sugar bowl and didn't like to ask, so she drank it as it was.

They had started playing and forgot her completely. It wasn't a pose. Nothing else existed for these three when they were making music. Sheila could have slipped off home and no one would have noticed. . . . The spell of the music fell on her, too.

They opened a magic door—a door through which Gino, too, could pass, to find happiness at the other side. She daren't think beyond that.

CHAPTER XI

What have I let myself in for? Sheila asked herself in the next few days. She was committed to this thing and she was determined to see it through. But never did a project bristle with such difficulties!

She decided it was the correct thing to mention it first of all to Sister Bain. She was so antagonistic towards Victor Cort. Sheila would never forget her look and tone as she spoke of 'poor heredity' and 'gipsy music—that sort of thing', the first time Gino's case came up. She had to be proved wrong about him. Also, of course, she always did her best for the children and was hardly likely to deny them the treat of an afternoon concert.

The Tatlows had offered two dates and Victor said he would fit in with either, whichever 'that bossy Ward Sister' chose. She picked the Thursday, pointing out that in point of fact any day during that fortnight would be equally inconvenient, they were going to be so short of staff. At Marbury General they had the 'block study' system, and just now the student nurses were withdrawn from ward duties for extra lectures and cramming before they sat their examination. Sister was against it. In her day they had got up early and put in an hour's study in their own rooms and lectures when they came off duty in the evening. She would rather see her girls at their practical work on the ward 'instead of doodling in the library or sunbathing on the roof'.

Sheila was bursting to point out that an afternoon concert was just the thing when they were short of nurses. The children would be so easy to manage. Sister foresaw that argument and said she had better bring out the big doll's house so that the little ones had some distraction when they got bored with the music. It wasn't going to be that kind of music, Sheila could have told her. Instead, she said meekly: 'Yes, Sister. And the colouring books.'

'I shall have to ask Matron's permission, of course,' said Sister Bain in a long-suffering tone.

Sheila hesitated. 'And it would be correct if I mentioned it to the Chief?'

'He'll approve, you may be sure,' snapped Sister Bain. 'Any excuse for turning the ward upside down!' She pursed her lips. 'He should be approached through the Registrar, as we're being so proper and correct. I leave that to you, Miss Thorne.'

I knew it, thought Sheila gloomily. If Red could put

a spoke in the wheel, he'd do that very thing. She began rehearsing a polite and formal request. There was one gleam of hope. Perhaps Lena had already issued her invitation to Mrs Devon. In that case, Red could hardly start raising objections now!

That afternoon Miss Furlong, good-hearted creature, popped in and read aloud a story to the solarium patients while the tinies had their nap and Sheila concentrated on young Stephen. They were working together through a set of test-papers which his form-master would mark at examination standard, as a guide to his progress. It was the geography paper they were tackling today, and a question on climate and weather in the western Mediterranean had them both bogged down.

Sheila confessed: 'I picture beautiful weather all the year round. The scent of orange blossom floating out to sea, fishing boats with picturesque sails, glorious beaches. . . . But of course, it was in the western Mediterranean, off Majorca, that the ships of the Carthaginian pirates were wrecked in a great winter storm, as we've been reading in your history course.'

Would she lose face if she confessed that her geography, like Sam Weller's acquaintance with London, was 'extensive and peculiar'—and as full of holes as a colander?

She saw Stephen's face light up. 'Hullo, Doctor Red. We're sunk.'

'Are you indeed!' He glanced at the rigging of Stephen's weights and pulleys and said sternly: 'And you with your royals up. That's bad seamanship. Remember the *Pamir*?'

He wasn't expected on the ward and in a minute the staff nurse would gallop up to attend him. Dare she mention the concert? Her neat little sentence had flown out of the window, his nearness made her pulses leap, colour stain her cheeks. How foolish to imagine he had made an excuse to look in, just because he was hungry for the sight of her!

Stephen was saying: 'We've run aground owing to bad weather in the western Mediterranean. Gale Force Ten at least.'

'Whew! That was some storm!' He caught sight of the test paper. 'Ah! You're putting me through a viva, are you? Well, here goes. The warm water of the Mediterranean in conjunction with the colder Atlantic winds may create numerous local storms and from January to March bad weather is frequent. Force Eight —gale force—quite common. Force Ten—storm force— possible now and then, say about once a month through the winter and early spring. Anything else? I once heard of a storm Force Fourteen in that sea, in midwinter. It sank a hundred ships up and down the coasts and will become legend. Fog is frequent with lower wind forces, especially around Gibraltar. Otherwise weather conditions vary a lot and can change rapidly. How am I doing?'

It was on Sheila that his eyes rested. And it wasn't just her fancy, there was a hunger in them, a reproach.

'Oh, boy, oh, boy!' said Stephen. 'We'll get full marks for that question.'

'I'm afraid we'll get no marks at all,' said Sheila in a tight little voice. 'It'd be cheating.'

As Red was cheating when he made love to her with his eyes, while all the time he and Ilse . . .

She couldn't bear it. She wanted to hit out, hurt him. *She'd show him.*

'I'd be so grateful, Doctor, if you'd mention to the Chief that we hope to put on a little concert for the children next Thursday afternoon. Victor Cort and some friends of his have very kindly offered——'

Long before she got so far his smile had gone out. Now he interrupted roughly: 'That fellow has the blasted cheek——'

A nurse in mauve stripes came hurrying up with a peculiar rolling, bouncing walk. Nurse Porson had charge of the ward this afternoon while Sister was off.

And from the opposite quarter strode Miss Furlong, looking upset and worried. Even more upset and worried when she found her ogre there, holding the deck, and at his most formidable.

'Oh, I beg your pardon, Doctor. There was a little matter I wanted to discuss with Miss Thorne. It will do another time. I believe I mustn't trouble her just now.' Backing away, flustered by his scowl, she dropped her storybook, and out of the pages fell a tuft of gay cock's feathers.

'What's this?' Red demanded. His attention was drawn to the thing by the hasty, furtive way Miss Furlong scooped it up and dropped it in her pocket, pretending she was hunting for a handkerchief. She did produce a handkerchief, but the feathers came out with it.

She murmured unhappily, 'This was under the pillow.' She appealed to Sheila. 'Bunty . . . the little girl with that distressing asthma . . . and so *thin*. Mrs Devon gives her special attention and I notice she has a foam rubber pillow instead of hair or feathers. So I did rather wonder if this was quite the best plaything. Of course '—she said this hastily, with half a glance at the ogre—' I'm in the dark on the clinical details. I remember a child called Evangeline who didn't react to any of the trigger tests.'

'She was allergic to her mum,' said Nurse Porson, being clever. And she in her turn looked at the Registrar, as if they shared a joke. His grim expression hardly bore that out. Nurse Porson said defensively: 'It isn't a plaything, anyway. It's a lucky charm. Velta has these little plumes of cock's feathers and parrot's feathers——'

'Lucky charm?' Red exploded. 'Are we back to the dark ages? What is Matron thinking about to let this ignorant girl loose on the patients?'

Sheila was on her feet, eyes blazing.

'That's unfair, and you know it. She's a splendid nurse.'

Red said grimly: 'Perhaps to you all medicine is just black magic?' As the nurse in mauve stripes giggled nervously, he swung round on her. 'This isn't a joke. It's damned superstitious nonsense.'

His angry glance passed over their faces: Sheila very flushed, Miss Furlong scandalized, Nurse Porson ready to burst into tears. With a sound of furious exasperation he stalked off.

Stephen said in an awed voice: 'Force Fourteen!'

It was too much to hope they'd hear no more about it. Nurse Porson could hardly wait for Sister to come on duty. She must have squeezed the last ounce of drama from the situation, Sheila thought, for Sister took it up with Matron, who brought in Sister Tutor and eventually poor Velta herself. That must have been quite a session, Sheila thought, all her sympathy with the girl. She had slipped her lucky charm under Bunty's pillow before she went off for her study fortnight. No, of course she hadn't meant any harm. Scraggy and wheezy though that poor mite was, and terribly difficult with her food, she loved her. She wept when they sternly told her that the precious little plume of magic feathers could have brought on a new and more dangerous attack of asthma.

Red came into it last of all. Sister was determined on a showdown. She simply wouldn't stand for his interference and his rudeness any longer. There was a terrific row. Sheila tiptoed past the office, hearing the raised, angry voices. What would be the outcome? It was the good old problem of an irresistible force meeting an immovable object—way beyond Stephen's mathematics or hers!

The office door was suddenly flung open. Red stalked out, angry and discomfited. He hadn't brought himself to apologize, and Sister Bain would be satisfied with nothing less. At any other moment it would have struck Sheila as comic that he chose to do it obliquely.

He planted himself in front of her, with Sister listening

to every word, for Sheila caught sight of her royal blue dress through the half-open office door.

'All right. So I misjudged the girl. You can have it all your way about her being a splendid nurse.'

'She really is, you know,' said Sheila. And off her own bat she added: 'And she isn't ignorant. She must have satisfied Matron in a written paper before she was accepted for the training school.'

From behind the office door Sister's voice joined in—just like the prison duet in *Il Trovatore*: 'And when she has her S.R.N. she'll be going back to do excellent work among her own people where every kind of medical help is so urgently needed.'

Sheila nipped in quickly. 'The girl who shares her room says she writes reams home every week. Practically a re-cap of the lectures!'

'With all this,' said Red sarcastically, 'it's unreasonable on my part to suppose she'd have the sense not to run round with lucky charms and lapse into island talk whenever she's excited.'

'Would you consider, Miss Thorne,' asked Sister in the same tone, 'that the language of rough sailors is suitable for children's ears?'

'Hell's bells!' raged the one-time ship's surgeon.

'You see what I'm up against, Miss Thorne,' said Sister Bain. 'And I believe seamen are very superstitious, too.'

It was defeat, and he knew it. The trouble is, thought Sheila, I'm really on his side. If I had a lucky charm handy, I'd wish . . .

On the corridor the loudspeaker system began buzzing.

'Doctor Redfern, please. Will Doctor Redfern please come to Minor Ops?'

But Sister Bain wouldn't let him off quite as easily as that. As he pushed the swing-doors, her raised voice followed him.

'Shall we go over the arrangements for Thursday's

concert, Miss Thorne? Matron is going to put on a lovely afternoon tea for Mr Cort and his friends.'

The doors swung viciously. Sheila stared after the tall figure with the blaze of red hair. She had that pang of emptiness and loss. *'What is all this sweet work worth, if thou kiss not me?'* Dr Redfern would certainly not be present at the concert.

✣   ✣   ✣

Concert was too dull and formal a word for that enchanting performance. Three people whose whole life was music sat there among the children and opened for them the door that led to magical delights. Everything seemed worth while—the worry and the scheming, the frantic last-minute chase round for a piano-tuner, even the secret dread that one of the children might suddenly come out with measles and the ward would have to be closed.

Gino watched the fiddle-bow as it flew over the strings or lingered on the exquisite double-stoppings of a folk-song or a wild gipsy dance.

They had gone through the programme, the children had clapped and cheered and whistled and Lena was gathering the music-sheets together, her husband putting his clarinet away in its case. Victor stepped forward a little, as he did on the stage. He was playing unaccompanied, his eyes on a little boy's face, playing for him alone. The ward was very still. The last notes hung on the air. Slowly the musician bent, one hand outstretched. Gino's hand slid into it.

Victor said softly: 'One of these days I'll teach you to play. Would you like that, boy? First you must learn how to hold the bow. So.' He was sitting on the edge of the bed, placing the child's fingers on the bow, making him curve the wrist. The two dark heads were close together. Then the man's arm was round the child. He was holding him tight, and neither of them needed to say a word.

A sob stuck in Sheila's throat. She had been absolutely tight all along. This was how it should be for Gino—now and always. If only Red were here to see the thing for himself. Was it the music that made her long for him so terribly at this moment?

She slipped away, leaving the father and child together. Matron was leading the special guests to partake of a delectable afternoon tea in the board-room. Dr Gannet had Frank Tatlow by the arm and Sheila heard him say earnestly: 'Do you recommend wooden or plastic recorders, if we persuade Miss Thorne to start a band?'

Another project! She might have known this would happen.

Lena was deep in talk with Mrs Devon. They left the ward side by side, Lena burdened with music. Victor and Frank took it for granted she would 'see to all that'.

From the ward kitchen came a lively clatter as the children's tea was got ready. Sheila glimpsed an orderly in green, two nurses stacking bread and butter at top speed. Mr Porson suddenly popped out. He'd been having a good old poke round, looking for trouble, as usual. Also he'd been helping himself to cake, and Sheila had caught him with his mouth full and a comical look of guilt.

He mumbled indistinctly: 'Entertainment is all very well, but it throws the nurses' rota out. They're put on already, goodness knows. All this fuss. And the kids kept waiting for attention.'

'I haven't heard the nurses complaining,' said Sheila, giving him a straight look.

Well, perhaps Nurse Porson had complained—through sheer force of habit—but the television fans had all wanted to stay on duty, and Sheila had seen them whip out their autograph books when Victor Cort arrived.

'They don't complain enough,' said Mr Porson, spluttering cake-crumbs.

Miss Furlong was right, Sheila thought. Joe Porson really was the most objectionable little man. It seemed a paradox that he should sacrifice valuable time—business hours and evenings he might have spent with his family—to sit through hospital committee meetings, consider tenders, view the new decorations or the handsome chip-range just installed in the cafeteria—and even attend a concert in the Children's Ward which he obviously considered a waste of everybody's time, including his own! Was it love of power, love of meddling? Or was there, deep down, some instinct to serve his fellow-men? There must be, though she found it hard to believe! There was something so baleful in the way he spat out: ' Slavedriving, that's what we're up against. And that's why Matron is always short of nurses.'

'But it's a very common problem these days, Mr Porson,' Sheila protested.

'We have special problems at Marbury General,' said Mr Porson significantly. 'We have, for instance, a certain young man who's asking for trouble. Big trouble. Orders the nurses round as if he were a consultant— which he's never likely to be if my vote counts. Talks big about rules and regulations, while all the time he's breaking rules himself.' He wagged a fat forefinger. 'People who live in glass houses shouldn't throw their weight around. And you can pass that on to your friend with my compliments.' He went lumbering off to join Matron's party.

Sheila pressed a hand to her burning cheek. *You can pass that on to your friend*. The threat in that was plain enough. Could this old humbug really make trouble for Red?

At that moment the Registrar came through the swing-doors. He stalked past her. She thought bitterly: So he deliberately cut the concert! He wasn't even at Scadcroft. And Joe Porson is right off the beam if he imagines we're close friends. What's the odd kiss?

He stopped, turned back, and said constrainedly: 'Sorry to miss your do.'

'Don't mention it, Doctor,' said Sheila, looking away.

He frowned. 'Now look. It wasn't deliberate. I was called to Casualty to admit a severely burnt child. I had to send him straight up to theatre and I've been standing by there. The outlook is grave.'

Sheila faltered: 'I didn't know. I thought——'

He took her hand. His fingers curled round hers, held on tightly.

'Why did you lie to me about Cort?' His voice held so much reproach and tenderness, it made her want to weep. 'Sheila, couldn't you trust me with the truth? It would have been kinder.'

'I did tell you the truth.'

A spasm of anger crossed his face. He let go her hand, thrust his own deep into the pockets of his white coat.

'Don't give me that! I'd have to be blind not to see how things are shaping. You let me think Cort was practically a stranger, when the fact is you meet at the Tatlows' house. She—the pianist—has been quite frank about it in speaking to Ilse.' All the gentleness was gone. He said harshly: 'Your friend has had quite a triumph, but it doesn't really change the situation. The child is precarious and needs to be kept under strict care. This sort of excitement is the worst thing for him, and if he reacts as I expect, I shall forbid visitors till he's on an even keel again.'

'No, it would be too cruel!' Sheila cried out. 'It's —it's just personal spite. You have no right to keep his father from him.'

'No?' said Red grimly.

She was speaking out of turn, but she felt reckless, beside herself. He was making nonsense of all she had worked for. 'There are things Gino needs even more than nursing care. He needs love. But you wouldn't understand that. You don't even *like* children. You only took this job because you wanted to turn the clock back. Victor tried to wipe out the past, too. But we can't, we can't! Life doesn't let us.'

The words tumbled out incoherently, she was half

weeping. It was intolerable that Ilse, who had treated his love so lightly in the past, should hold his whole future in her hand. Then the enormity of what she had said came home to her and she clapped a trembling hand to her mouth.

She saw his face, tormented with regret and pain, and then a mask seemed to fall over his features. His voice came clipped and formal.

'Anything more?'

'Forgive me,' whispered Sheila. 'I didn't mean what I said.'

'But it's true,' he said.

She stood there, feeling empty and lifeless, till he had gone from her sight.

CHAPTER XII

When Red appeared on the ward, everyone jumped to it, and today was no exception. It was a hectic moment. The children, mouse-quiet during the concert, were letting off steam, calling out for attention and bouncing on their beds or rattling cot-sides. Two student nurses hurried round with bowls and towels, sprucing them up for tea. But there was a corner of the ward where tense quiet reigned. A cubicle was being prepared for the severely burnt and shocked child who would presently be brought down from theatre, and Red was organizing the blood transfusion, with his houseman haring round for a bit of apparatus that was missing.

Red wasn't the man to direct operations from a distance. He was in the thick of the fight for this child's life. It tortured Sheila to think that no matter how terrifically he worked, his career could be jeopardized by that insufferable Mr Porson, who was sniffing round after hospital scandals in his pre-election zeal. Then she told herself Dr Gannet wouldn't let that happen. He had stood up to Mr Porson and Mr Mercks over the appointment of a ward teacher, and he would be a lion in defence of his Registrar.

But even if he took a strong line with old Porson, Ilse might get to hear of it, and suffer deeply. Wouldn't the niece take a spiteful pleasure in hinting to the woman she disliked, and whom she had called the Black Widow, that there were other spiders and other parlours? Sheila found the idea sickening. Ilse had been friendly and kind. And Red loved her. From the very beginning, when she chose his friend and he had taken his broken heart to sea, she had been the one and only woman for him and he had proved it by coming back to her, taking any job that offered and making a go of it. Could there be any doubt in the world about the outcome? Perhaps Ilse was slow in making up her mind; perhaps Red wanted to wait till she was absolutely sure. But in the end they would accept the second chance Fate offered.

Ilse must never know that he'd been disloyal, that he had yielded to the temptation of wild music and a starlit night. It was a memory Sheila was determined to forget. Then she'd come face to face with him, round the corner of the day, and it would all come rushing back—the achingly sweet pain of being crushed in his arms, the passionate kisses and the unsteadily whispered words. She was remembering it now, in spite of all her resolution. It made her tremble with longing.

'Gangway!' A brisk young nurse steered the trolley past her, all the tea-things rattling.

She went to find Victor. He was still with Gino. The little boy had snuggled up to his father and they were talking together in low voices, happy nonsense, stories from Victor's travels, dreams for the journeys they would make together.

'A musician's hands,' Victor said, looking at the small fingers that lay confidingly in his. 'But it's hard work, boy! You won't love me when I make you stick at your bowing and you're wanting to run out and play with the other kids. And I warn you there'll be corns on these finger-tips!'

Sheila thought with anguish: He still doesn't accept what Red told him. Gino won't be running out to play, and slogging away at music practice will be way beyond his strength. He mustn't promise these things!

Perhaps Victor saw this in her face. He took possession of her hand, studying the finger-tips with mock gravity.

'What are we to make of this? No corns, just a little hardness. That means she plays the guitar. Right? And make no mistake about it, boy, the guitar is a very fine instrument. Isn't it the lovers' friend on a starry night? Think of Segovia. He can fill the Royal Festival Hall. Think of Django Reinhardt. He could hold any crowd spellbound. A gipsy guitarist with a crippled hand—but when he and Stephane Grapelly got together at the Hot Club de France, I tell you they made music. God, these crummy, tone-deaf kids with a bit of polished wood and an amplifier and three chords! They call that playing the guitar, and the girls squeal like little pigs.'

Gino, big-eyed, mouse-quiet, hung on his words.

'I'll make another guess,' Victor said. 'She brought her guitar to the party and no one asked her to play. But she shall play for us now. We insist absolutely.'

Gino babbled: 'It's a real Spanish guitar with red ribbons!'

The children all began clamouring, to Sheila's burning mortification; for she was aware that Red, gowned and masked over there in the isolation cubicle, was looking in their direction. She freed her hand with a sharp tug.

'The concert is over.' She gave Victor a look of urgent appeal. 'All the visitors have gone and we're in the way of the nurses. Matron's tea-party will fall very flat, too, I'm afraid, if the chief guest isn't there!'

Victor stood up reluctantly. 'Very well, I'll come quietly.' He rumpled Gino's hair. 'I'll be seeing you tomorrow, boy, before I go back to London.' His voice had gone rough and uneven. He went out with long strides, not looking back, and unaware of the smiling, hopeful glances of the nurses as he passed. Beyond the swing-doors he halted and turned to face Sheila. His eyes were full of tears.

'God, to go away and leave him there. . . . It's all wrong. We should be together. I want to make up for the lost years. That fool of a doctor is talking through his hat when he says . . .' He couldn't go on. After a moment he mastered himself, hunched his shoulders. 'As for their blasted tea-party . . .' He laughed bitterly. 'Nothing doing.'

Sheila said urgently: 'The concert has gone so well, it would be a mistake to offend Matron and Doctor Gannet.'

'Tell them this place gets me down and the tea would choke me.' It was true he had gone quite ghastly pale. At that moment the lift-doors opened. A porter and a theatre nurse appeared wheeling a stretcher, while a surgeon in green theatre garb walked alongside keeping a check on the drip apparatus which was clamped to the stretcher. Sheila was quite used to such sights by now, but the effect on Victor was shattering. He flattened himself against the wall, putting up both hands to his face.

'Giovanna! It was just like this. I was waiting in the corridor and the stretcher passed me. They wouldn't let me be with her, they were afraid of some infection in her weak state. And when they let me in, it was only because she was dying——' Face ravaged and working, voice hoarse, he said: 'I must get Gino away from this place. Do you understand?' He rushed out, the doors flapping after him.

Yes, she understood, and her heart ached with pity.

She went laggingly to Matron's room where a clatter of tea-things and a pleasant ripple of talk met her. People looked round expectantly and she had to explain that Mr Cort begged to be excused as he was feeling unwell.

She understood that, too. He was sick with *those things whereof our conscience is afraid*. He blamed himself for abandoning Giovanna's baby son, blamed himself for the Browns' neglect of the child and for the illness which had landed him here in hospital. Tomorrow she must make it absolutely clear that these things were not his fault. And remorse was so wasteful, so destroying. He must look forward, and she would stand by him, no matter what it cost her. Even as she thought this, she knew what a burden she was taking upon her heart.

But tomorrow, though she and Gino watched for him eagerly, he didn't appear. Or the next day, or the next. The little boy had stood the excitement of the concert very well, but now she saw him begin to flag. Before her eyes he seemed to grow smaller, his features sharper, the eyes enormous and filled with a silent reproach and dread. From his chart she saw that his pulse was slower, his temperature up. She arrived one morning to find he had been isolated on Red's orders. Dr Gannet made a round that day and was a long time at Gino's bedside. He was seen off the ward with the usual ceremony and Red stood talking to the houseman. They were near enough to Sheila for their words to reach her clearly.

'Right,' Dick Sawley was saying. 'I'll do a Mantoux test, but it'll take a few weeks to develop.'

'And it may not be positive, even then.' Red rubbed a hand distractedly through his hair. 'I can't find Kernig's sign. But again, that might be absent. A lumbar puncture would clinch it, though I don't want to put the little chap through all that for nothing. If I've missed something, God help me!'

Nurse Velta was walking up and down, crooning a fretful child to sleep in her arms. She gave Sheila a significant look, rolling up her eyes. 'I sure done go slip ma magic feathers under that chile's pillow when I done make his bed! Oh, lordy, yes!'

Sheila felt distracted with worry and uncertainty—and

she couldn't get Gino out of her mind, though goodness knows it wasn't for lack of other worries! Mr Dee had sent a message about a child hurt in a car smash, and she skipped coffee break to go down to Outpatients, where the orthopaedic surgeon and Dr Gannet had rooms at opposite ends of the pleasant reception hall, with the eye specialist's department and the fracture room in between. She had tapped at Mr Dee's door when she saw Mrs Brown come out of Dr Gannet's room, a handkerchief to her eyes, and hurry away. That made Sheila's heart drop like a stone. Had Mrs Brown come along of her own accord, had she news of Victor? Or had the Chief sent for her, and did that mean . . . Mr Dee's secretary opened the door. Ilse was there, too, and they discussed the new case.

The accident had occurred at a remote country place and there had been a dramatic dash by ambulance, escorted by police car, to get the injured child and his parents to hospital.

' The child was in the back seat. His legs were trapped and he has a dislocated shoulder, but he'll be all right. Unluckily, the parents came off worse, they're still unconscious and of course they'll be unable to visit the laddie for quite some time. That's why I want you to combine plenty of distraction, lessons, games, whatever you can lay on, with the physiotherapy, so that Philip doesn't lose any use in that injured arm. Right?' He beamed at them both. ' Splendid teamwork, splendid!'

' Teamwork,' repeated Ilse Devon, when she and Sheila were out in the waiting hall again. Her voice was bitter. ' Right up in the clouds, isn't he? And the Chief, too.'

Her voice was unfriendly, even hostile.

' We'll do what we can for Philip,' Sheila said hesitantly.

' Oh, of course I shall exercise that arm. Hamish Dee doesn't have to teach me my job! And you may be sure the nurses will pet and spoil him. But lessons—when he's all tensed up and worried about his parents—well, really!'

'So is Gino tensed up and worried,' blurted Sheila. 'And it'll be worse now he's isolated. Why had Red to do that?'

'Oh, he has this thing about infections,' said Ilse, her tone light, her eyes wary. 'They all have a bee in their bonnet about *something*. Dr Gannet will never rest till they build a new block where mothers can be admitted with their children and look after them all day long— no matter what happens to the family! Failing that, he'd close the unit and have us running round treating the children at home. And Hamish Dee has a craze for getting fracture patients mobile. He'd have me giving them walking practice between the parallel bars when they can hardly stand. And Red '—she paused—' he's afraid of overlooking something.'

'But Gino will fret and make himself worse.'

'You can give him news of his father,' said Ilse.

'What makes you think that?'

Ilse opened her eyes wide. 'From what Mrs Tatlow said——'

All because she had stitched a loose button on Victor's coat, Sheila thought vexedly. It was just wishful thinking. Lena and Frank so much wanted Victor to settle down, and especially now that Gino needed a home. She said stonily: 'I have no news from Victor at all.'

They began walking down the hall, past the receptionist at her desk which had flowers and magazines on it, past the snack bar in the corner. Ilse put a hand on Sheila's arm and said: 'Forgive me. I know the separation is hard on you both.'

Sheila stood still and faced her. It was a time for plain speaking. She said in a rush: 'You've got quite the wrong idea. There's nothing like that between us.'

Ilse insisted: 'But it *was* on Victor Cort's account you were so dreadfully upset that night I found you wandering in the rain?'

Sheila flushed. 'Oh, that! Yes, I was worried, but not in the way you mean. You're absolutely on the wrong track.'

Ilse gave a little laugh. 'Do you know, at the time I thought you were in a state because Dick Sawley had to pass up your date. Dick has such a way with him!'

Sheila said steadily: 'We're friends—I hope. He's going to the nurses' dance with Eileen Connell on Saturday, and I think that's a splendid idea.'

'Are you being noble—or have you found another boy-friend?' Ilse's tone was still light, but the line of her jaw was tense and her hands were crisped up tightly. 'I'm the soul of discretion, Sheila dear, if you want to confide in me.'

This is it, Sheila was thinking. Every nerve cried danger. Ilse had her suspicions, and perhaps her whole future happiness—and Red's—depended on this moment. So she found courage to look the other woman in the eye and say: 'Didn't I tell you, right at the start, I'm not interested in boy-friends? I'm far too keen on my job to bother with that sort of thing.' She saw the tenseness go out of Ilse in a long, sighing breath. And because of the sick pain in her heart as she told that lie, because of the longing to be in Red's arms and at his side, now and always, proudly, before the whole world, she went on talking very fast on the way back to the ward. 'This boy, Philip, is from the country. I wonder if he has green fingers? We've been growing seeds and the little plants are just ready to prick out for our window-boxes. If we could find some way of letting him do that in bed——'

She found a chance at teatime to catch Dick Sawley alone and ask him point-blank what was happening to Gino.

He said guardedly: 'He's on penicillin and we're doing a skin test.'

Sheila nerved herself. 'Just what is that for?'

A voice behind her said: 'For T.B.' It was Red at his

most formidable. Dick Sawley, in a hurry to get from underfoot, drank off his tea scalding hot, an expression of anguish appeared on his face and he bolted. Sheila scarcely noticed that he had gone, she was so shocked, and stared at Red in bewilderment.

'We've nothing definite to go on,' Red told her. 'We knew the mother was delicate, and now Mrs Brown mentions her thinness, the cough. I've got to make certain before we can rule it out. This last relapse worries me.'

'He's fretting for his father, it's as simple as that, though you're trying to make it all so complicated! Oh, I know for certain fear and worry can make a child ill, the body and the mind aren't separate things. Look at Evangeline Hobbs.'

'Not again!' said Red in mock alarm, his grim expression relaxed for a moment.

Sheila said thoughtfully: 'Now I know why Mrs Brown looked so upset.'

'Put yourself in her place. She has young children. If the test is positive, it would be risky having Gino with them.'

'But there isn't any question of his going back to the Browns,' Sheila said intensely.

'His father is making other arrangements? We're in the dark, of course, but no doubt you get news regularly.' His voice was grim again; it held anger and impatience. 'Well?' His eyes bored down into hers.

Sheila looked away. 'It isn't easy to get in with the recording companies and he must have drawn a blank so far. But I know he's trying desperately hard.' Her throat went tight. 'I only hope he won't despair.'

Above her head Timothy Redfern said softly: 'Oh, my dear heart, why must you make it so hard for yourself? Isn't it time you gave some man the right to take care of you and do all the worrying?' The change was so sudden, his tenderness was so much harder to endure than his anger, she gave him a wild startled look, forcing herself to remember that every word he spoke was disloyal to Ilse.

Sister Bain put her head out of the office. '*If* you want a cup of tea, Doctor——' she said crossly.

A day or two later, Lena Tatlow came wandering round looking for her. She had been to the physiotherapy department for treatment. 'A bit of pain and stiffness in this wretched arm. I've been overdoing it, I suppose. All the music-copying, and on top of that I've been playing for a dancing class.' She laughed. 'You know. Strumming away, tonic and dominant, for hours at a stretch. . . . But the money's useful. We never know when the variety theatre may close down and then things'll be tight. The musician's life!' She gave Sheila a quick look and hurried on: 'If Doctor Gannet is still plugging away at the idea of recorders for the children, Frank has several types. Drop in for coffee some evening and have a look at them, will you?'

'I'd love to. We've got a percussion band started, and as a matter of fact we're practising secretly for Sister's birthday. We have one or two children who played recorders at school, so we might work up something in time.' That tailed off. She met Lena's eyes. 'I've thought a few times of dropping in to see if you had news of Victor.'

'Not a sausage. But surely he's writing to you? Phoning?' The whimsical flicker of amusement again. 'Reversing the charges, as usual!' But when she found that Sheila had no news, the smile faded. She stood there, her face drawn into worried lines, automatically rubbing the stiff hand. 'I can't believe it! He was obsessed by the idea of making a home for Gino, and it was quite obvious he thought the world of you. . . . Sheila, have we been just blundering fools? Try to forgive us. And do drop in, just the same. There's always plenty of coffee. And washing up!'

Sheila faced the thing out. Victor wasn't coming back. The wandering life had taken hold of him again. She was stricken to the heart—not for her own sake, Lena and Frank were wildly off the mark there—but because the dream she had planted in a little boy's heart would never flower after all.

❖   ❖   ❖

Easter had fallen early, in bleak, hearth-hugging weather; but Whitsun brought May sunshine and soft breezes. Sheila spent a week by the sea with her parents, filling the empty, sunny hours by walking miles along the cliff tops, where the nesting frenzy of a host of terns and kittiwakes went on all around her. It was the longest week of her life.

The first person she saw on her return to the hospital was Timothy Redfern. Her heart seemed to jar and then race crazily. During that long week's absence she had read her own heart; she loved him hopelessly and for ever, and it all led nowhere. If it hadn't been too crazy a notion, she'd have imagined he was waiting around by the porter's box on some flimsy excuse, just to see her. His eyes flew to hers, seemed to dwell hungrily on every line of her face. Then the spell was broken effectively, for he turned to the porter and said crisply: 'Never mind, he can't have got to the office yet. When you get a reply will you tell Mr Niblett that if three o'clock at his place is no good, Mrs Devon and I will expect him at the flat round about seven tonight?'

Then he fell into step with Sheila and said: 'I don't need to ask if you had good weather, I can see you had! You needed that holiday. This job takes too much out of you—or you put too much into it—and I was going to suggest a check-up with your doctor. A blood-count. At a rough guess I'd say you were eighty-two instead of in the nineties.'

A sort of rage took hold of Sheila. That blue, deep-sea gaze which had reached out to her with such intensity didn't mean he had missed her. He was just weighing up whether she was anaemic! She laughed a little stridently. 'Don't start on me! I refuse to be a guinea-pig like poor little Gino.'

Red said constrainedly: 'Gino is in the clear. Back on the balcony. His test was negative.'

'I could have told you that long ago,' said Sheila.

They had passed under the old brick archway and down the covered passage to the yard, with doors and stone steps leading into the complicated mole-run of the admin building which faced the street. It was a few yards from here, that Friday night, that Red had taken her in his arms, and the memory was too much for her. She couldn't see straight or think straight. She had to lash out and hurt him.

'You have to track down every sign and symptom. Is it to prove to the Chief that you're *with* it? Or is it because you don't see a child as a person, but only as a machine with all sorts of fiddly bits that can go wrong and . . . and provide you with an interesting detective puzzle? Gino must have been a godsend!'

'You couldn't possibly,' said Red in a bitter voice, 'put it more neatly.'

He went clattering up the stone steps and left her to cross the yard alone.

That morning Gino's parcel came. It was postmarked Vienna and bore an imposing customs declaration. In a perfect haystack of shavings and tissue paper nestled a little carved house with a hinged roof. You opened the roof and wound a key at the back, and it played three delicate little folk tunes while two gaily painted gipsy dolls an inch tall danced round and round, the tiny man with a fiddle under his chin, the tiny lady holding an accordion. Their legs were fine wire pins and it was the vibration of the music that made them dance, gazing at one another like lovers under a spell. It was an enchanting toy and it lifted Gino into a seventh heaven of delight.

'No message?' said Ilse, clearing the decks for an exercise session. 'But of course, there's no point in sending letters to a child who doesn't read or write!

What is the man doing in Vienna? Don't tell me you haven't a clue!' She smiled in a certain way.

'There's a festival of popular music. He may have an engagement there. I didn't even know he was abroad.'

Ilse's smile held polite unbelief. She could afford to smile, Sheila thought mutinously. Who was Mr Niblett, and what business had Red and Ilse with him 'at the flat round about seven tonight'?

'Now then, children,' Ilse was saying briskly, 'put away your bits of nonsense, lie flat on your backs, hands down by your sides, and get ready to flop like a jelly——'

Gino had made no sign of listening to their conversation, but that morning he didn't content himself with drawing matchstick men who performed all he saw going on round him in the ward. He toiled away at his sums and his letters like the other children. His hands were clammy with the struggle, and when his pencil point snapped under fierce pressure there was a storm of tears and 'monkey language'. Sheila made time later to come back to him and they had a reading lesson. But in the back of her mind was a nagging doubt. With sweat and tears Gino could achieve a thank-you letter for his magic toy—but would Victor ever receive it? Wasn't he on his travels again by now, his conscience stilled by the gift of the musical box, while the child waited and hoped?

In a few days he was allowed up in his dressing-gown and took Jackie's place as Sheila's monitor, fetching and carrying for her, proud to be singled out. Once when she missed him, she found him cross-legged on the storeroom floor. He had got her guitar out of its case and was plucking the strings softly, rapt and absorbed. Sister was cross. He'd been so ill, and to be in and out of draughts and actually sitting in that cold store-room!

'Couldn't he help Stephen with that model yacht he's making, or is it too fiddly? If Gino has one of his tantrums and smashes the thing, it will be too grieving.'

That was up to Stephen. When he agreed, the little boy was so proud to help—if it was merely sorting out balsa wood of the right length or cautiously opening another tube of glue—that Sheila felt his recovery had taken another stride forward. Now that he was busy and happy, the physical improvement was sensational. She had every right to say 'I told you so!' to an over-zealous Registrar, but she was keeping out of his way. They had been a whole week without exchanging a single word!

She had thankfully put away Stephen's maths books and was admiring the progress of the model yacht one afternoon when she saw Red come in with a grey-haired, weathered man in the uniform of a captain of the Merchant Navy.

Stephen looked across the ward and said excitedly: 'Oh, boy, oh, boy! That's Captain Foley. He was Red's skipper and he's coming to look at my boat, what do you think of that, miss?'

Sheila said she thought it was splendid and made hasty preparations to depart. But a nurse hurried in and called Red to the phone; Captain Foley was left there on his own, very much at sea in the big ward. Sheila could do no other but go across and say with a shy smile: 'Captain Foley? There's a boy over here with a boat nearly ready for launching.'

A moment later Captain Foley was examining the little yacht, of which the hull was completed and the mast and rigging just at a delicate stage. 'She's a half-decked centre-board sloop,' volunteered Stephen.

'Bermudan-rigged?' said Captain Foley, as one sailor to another.

'You bet, sir!'

'She'll race well.'

Captain Foley was a Devon man and there was that lovely burr on his voice as he spoke of yacht racing in Dawlish Bay. And then he had the two boys hanging breathlessly on his words, yarning about the ocean-going yacht he had skippered for a millionaire in his younger days. The sight of two gauze-masked nurses with a dressings trolley brought him up short.

'I'll tack about and find that young man of mine!' He smiled down at Stephen. 'He tells me you'll soon be nifty on your pins again and able to sail your boat. Good luck to you, Stephen! You'll be going to sea one of these days?'

'You bet I will, sir. I've talked it over with Doctor Red and I'm going to be a marine engineer, but it means the heck of a lot of maths!'

They shook hands on it. Captain Foley rumpled Gino's dark hair. 'And are you going to be a greaser, too, laddie?'

Gino was torn for a moment. But only for a moment. His head went up, his eyes flashed with pride.

'I'm going to be a musician. And my dad is going to take me all round the world with him. He promised.'

A spasm of pain crossed Captain Foley's face. 'Your dad is a lucky man.' He turned aside.

Nurse Porson was in charge of the dressings trolley. Sheila heard her say to the student helping her: 'Some world cruise that'll be! Busking for theatre queues or fiddling away in little bars. And with an invalid child cramping his style.'

Sheila felt hotly angry. She thought Gino was too busy with the boat to overhear the cruel words, the nurses chattered all the time and it just merged with the background like that blaring radio which had got on her nerves so much at first. All the same, Nurse Porson had to be ticked off. It would be a pleasure! But she had to delay it while she saw Captain Foley off the ward, for Red had obviously been called down to Outpatients where the orthopaedic clinic was taking place at this time.

As they crossed the ward together, the burly man with the four wide rings of gold braid on his sleeve said to her in a voice gruff with feeling: 'It gets me. Tim Redfern throwing up the sea and giving his life to these children, just because——' He looked sideways at her. 'He's told you? About my little chap?'

Sheila shook her head. She had gone a little pale, dreading what was coming next, yet burningly eager for the truth.

'You have a family?'

'We had just one little boy—late-born, when we'd given up hope of a child. He was the pride of our hearts, I could hardly bear to be parted from him. And when he was two years old, I persuaded my wife to bring the little chap with her on a voyage to the East. We had a ship's surgeon and that helped Mrs Foley to decide. She knew I thought a lot of our young medico, who had served in my ship for two years—ever since he qualified, in fact.'

They had reached the swing-doors, the short corridor was deserted, quiet, secret. Perhaps that helped a man of few words to pour out his heart now: the sorrow and grief long hidden away came out like the easing of a wound.

'The trouble was, of course, Tim had no experience with children, beyond the three months he'd done here, as a student. And anyway, it's not the sort of work you expect aboard a cargo vessel! When my boy seemed off-colour, fretful and off his food, on the trip home, half way across the Indian Ocean, Tim put it down to the heat, then to some tummy upset. When he got worse he began to think it might be typhoid. But he was wrong. It was meningitis. Out of sheer inexperience, not neglect, he missed some sign which might have told him the truth.'

Sheila stood shocked and still, the tears unashamed in her eyes.

Captain Foley said in that gruff voice: 'Within a week my boy was dead. And it's an agonizing thing to witness, though Tim did every mortal thing to give the child ease. He was fearless in his work, you know, and

I guess he still is. I've seen him amputate a seaman's foot that got caught in a steel hawser—passed him the instruments and marvelled at his precision and coolness, with the ship pitching and the lamp swinging overhead. I've seen him give a couple of Lascars holy murder for slicing one another up in a knife-fight. But the loss of that child broke him, he was stricken to the heart. He blamed himself; though even if he'd made the right diagnosis, I don't believe the outcome would have been different—so far from land, and without the sort of thing he needed in such a desperate case. Mrs Foley and I wrestled with the thing and accepted it as God's will. But not Red. He quit at the end of the trip, got them to rub out his contract and came back to hospital, under a Chief whose work he trusted; said he was going to force him to create a job, if there wasn't one available, and work the thing out of his system by hard sweat.'

He paused, hesitated. 'I know there were personal reasons why he'd never intended coming back to Marbury. But that was something he had to take in his stride in order to work under Doctor Gannet.' He smiled suddenly. 'He's as stubborn as the devil, and we had blazing rows, but his integrity is absolute. He steers by the stars.'

He steers by the stars. Those words haunted Sheila long after Dick Sawley had appeared and taken Captain Foley in tow, long after school was over and she had walked home through the park, they were with her still as she lay sleepless that night with all the stars of heaven blazing down at her through her window. She knew it to be true, and she burned with shame, remembering the bitter things she had said to Red about his fussiness over Gino.

And what Captain Foley had revealed took her even further into a young doctor's heart and mind. He had come back to Marbury General with a purpose. His inexperience had perhaps cost a child's life and he was determined to make sure that never happened again. It wasn't for Ilse's sake he had come back. Everyone, including Ilse herself, had taken it for granted, but it wasn't true. And the knowledge set wild new hopes beating in her heart.

She scarcely slept. Her mother exclaimed in dismay when she appeared at the breakfast table with dark smudges under her eyes, and couldn't get a mouthful down.

'I wish you hadn't to go to that place today, Sheila. I wish you could take it easy at home—and make your father do the same. He's come back from his holiday determined to get the garden in order, and I can't get him to slow down! Couldn't I ring Doctor Gannet?'

'Against all the rules of etiquette?' Sheila exclaimed in horror. 'I'm all right. It's a wonderful job, I love every minute of it!' And never had there been a morning so full of promise, with larks singing and the air scented with May blossom, never had her step been so light.

But as she pushed open the swing-doors of the ward, she sensed calamity. Matron herself was there, grave-faced, consulting with Sister Bain. And it was Sister who stepped forward and gave her the news.

'Gino has disappeared.'

CHAPTER XIII

'Gino has . . . Oh, no!'

Nurse Connell, in tears, protested: 'Wasn't the spalpeen in the corner of me eye the whole blessed time?'

'Obviously he wasn't,' Matron said sternly.

There was one thing about Sister Bain, she stood by her nurses.

'We can keep tabs on the children in bed, Matron, but once they're ambulant they're up to their monkey tricks. I must say the active ones have been under control since

we had a ward teacher. But it was during the breakfast
lark that Gino seems to have slipped away. You know
the tinies and the fracture cases need a lot of help with
their meals, and I'm so short of nurses——'

Her voice was calm; her distress of mind was shown
only by the blotches of colour on neck and brow—as if,
Sheila thought, Norina had been at her with a paintbox.
But she was annoyed rather than scared. Only for
Sheila had this delicious, dancing May morning suddenly
shed all its brightness.

'He must be somewhere,' Matron said. 'You remember the scare we had over Jackie? We'd just called the
police when he was found fast asleep on the top shelf of
the blanket cupboard, having climbed up by a table
and a pile of linen that had since been moved.'

'The blanket cupboard,' said Sister Bain, 'was the
first place I looked. We've searched everywhere,
Matron.'

Nurse Velta was in fact hanging over the balcony,
peering down past the bird-tray and the window-boxes.
She came hurrying to report.

'There ain't no place more to look, Sister ma'am.
Gino done gone for sure.' She rolled eyes of woe. 'And
this here sharp little calypso box done gone, too.'

For Sheila, at least, that settled it. This was no game
of hide and seek. Gino had taken his treasure with him.

'Very well, Sister. I'll have the whole building
searched.'

And Matron might well be dismayed at the prospect.
This old building was full of nooks and crannies. There
was the yard, the huts which housed special departments,
the boiler-house and stores, the basement. And of course
there was the old brick archway which art students came
to sketch, and which led straight on to a busy street of the
city. Perhaps that was in all their minds.

Matron said: 'Oh, the child can't just have walked
out into the street in his hospital dressing-gown. And a
musical box under his arm!'

But he could, Sheila thought, if he had overheard Nurse Porson's senseless, cruel words yesterday and turned them over in that fanciful brain of his.

Matron met the Ward Sister's eye. 'Doctor Gannet ought to be told.'

'He's down with 'flu, Matron. Or at least it's a feverish cold which might turn out to be 'flu.'

And that, of course, made him unapproachable. Dick Sawley had told Sheila with a straight face that if the Chief sneezed once the ward had to be disinfected. And if he sneezed twice it was panic stations, with Mrs Gannet cutting the telephone wires and barring their front door, while dear Alexander lay snug in bed sipping whisky and hot milk and catching up on the medical journals. And all, of course, because he was afraid of passing on germs to the children. The look Matron and Sister Bain exchanged conveyed that today it was providential.

'And Doctor Redfern?'

'He's at Scadcroft the whole day, Matron, with Mrs Devon. A big after-care session.'

Yes, Sheila remembered now, they had been talking about it yesterday, and Ilse had promised to deliver the powder colour and brushes she had got ready for Norina.

'I can get him on the phone, of course, Matron.'

Matron said carefully: 'We'll have a big search made first. We don't want a big fuss and the police dragged into it.'

'Quite, Matron.'

For that red-headed doctor would certainly go to town on a slip-up like this. Talk about throwing his weight around!

Sheila was following her own train of thought. 'Could you just make sure no stranger has been in, Sister?'

Sister Bain's eyes popped. 'His father! But I thought he was abroad? And in any case, he wouldn't dare.' Her cheeks were bright red with outrage.

Sheila said draggingly: 'I know it sounds crazy. But

Doctor Redfern did tell him he would refuse permission for the child to leave hospital. And then again things have been said about him going out to Scadcroft or being returned to the Browns.' She added silently: *Red, darling Red, forgive me! It's the truth or nothing now. For Gino's sake. He's in danger.*

Sister Bain looked hard at the ward teacher. 'He had the child's welfare at heart.'

Matron put in irritably: 'Come now, Sister. Let's get a move on.'

It took only a couple of minutes to establish that there had indeed been a stranger on the ward: dark, rough-looking, in a brown overall. They had taken him for a new porter and he had gone off with a big armload of stretcher blankets. Of course, they'd been too busy to pay much attention. . . . No autograph books for Victor Cort this morning, Sheila thought bitterly.

'It's an outrage,' said Sister Bain, her cheeks bright red now.

'There may really be a new porter,' Matron pointed out. 'I'll quickly find out. We'll handle this from my office, I think.' And she began to lead the way. Sister Bain, following her, met Sheila's eyes.

'That child needs such care. He can't take any rough handling or excitement.' Her eyes held urgency.

Matron was saying briskly over her shoulder: 'We'll continue the search all over the building, of course. But if the child has actually been kidnapped, the sooner we get the police on to it the better.'

Sheila watched them out of sight, then she nipped back into the cloakroom where she had just left her coat and handbag. Thank goodness it was Miss Furlong's day. A few moments later she was hurrying across the yard, out by a side gate and making for the taxi-rank.

It was Lena who opened the door to her, and her face showed tremendous relief.

'Victor was absolutely sure you'd come. The whole plan is geared to that. Only, of course, he daren't let you know in advance, that was the awkward thing. He was so afraid you'd give the thing away by last-minute preparations.' She was moving towards the music-room door as she spoke.

'Wait.' Sheila pointed to the telephone in the hall. 'Ring the hospital. Now. At once. Ask for Matron's office. Her secretary will take the call. Tell her I'm with Gino and he's safe and well. Then ring off quickly before Matron gets on the blower herself and asks a million questions.' Later, she'd have to think out how the affair could be presented to Matron in a way that made sense at all. She knew already that Red would never accept it. A hot anger filled her when she thought of Victor's folly in snatching the child away like that, after the months and months of care and treatment. Worse still, he had counted on her to back him up!

Yet when she opened the door of the big front room, her heart smote her. For to these people, living in their world of music with only contempt for the values set on material things, all this *did* make sense.

The room was as untidy as ever. There was a row of recorders of different sizes and types, alongside Frank's clarinet and saxophone; music scattered everywhere; the eternal pot of coffee on top of the stove and beside it a plate of cinnamon toast, cold and unappetizing. But there was also Gino wrapped up in blankets on a studio couch, his face absolutely radiant. He looked so fragile: candle-flame in the wind, blossom on the bough, a sigh would carry him away. He had the musical box in front of him and his father was holding him tightly.

Before Sheila could speak he said defiantly: 'It was the only way, and you know it. That doctor would never have let him go to me, though the Browns could have had him back like a shot.'

'When he was fit. And that won't be for a long time yet,' said Sheila with a most urgent, imploring look. 'Believe me, Doctor Redfern knows all the risk, and there's nothing in his mind but the child's future.'

'And what's in Mrs Brown's mind? I can tell you,' said Victor savagely. 'Five hundred pounds. I've been to see her and I got the whole sorry tale of Brown's investment in a "nice little business" that was on its last legs when he took over. A house-shop in the middle of old property due for demolition. I ask you! And that was where Gino was brought up.' He got to his feet and began pacing with a furious restlessness. 'When she saw me billed at the variety theatre Mrs Brown began visiting the hospital again. They figured out that if they took the child back, I'd be so darned grateful, I wouldn't start asking awkward questions about the money.' His eyes glinted. 'It's the other way round. If they so much as lay a finger on my boy, I sue them for my five hundred pounds.'

'Fade-out of the Browns,' said Lena dryly.

Sheila could find it in her heart to pity the Browns. With them, nothing ever turned out for the best. They had wanted Victor's motherless babe, but he had been displaced in their affection by children of their own; the money must have seemed a godsend, too, but it had been swallowed up by a luckless investment, and after all their work and worry to keep the little shop open, Brown had had to go back to his trade. Then Gino's long illness had complicated things. It was only when she remembered how they had thrown the toy violin in the ashbin and made Victor out to be a shiftless rogue that she felt the old indignation rise up in her again.

Frank, smiling in his vague, shy way, said: 'We have other ideas for Gino's future. Isn't it high time you broke the news to Sheila—considering how closely it concerns her? How about washing up the breakfast things, Lena, and making fresh coffee?'

Lena didn't need a second hint to leave Sheila and Victor together. At the door she remarked: 'Why don't we eat off vine-leaves like the Greeks? You gobble up your plate and there's no washing up at all!'

Victor had his back turned. As the door closed, he

swivelled round. He had brought out an old leather wallet. 'Look what I hold in my hand: Gino's future—and ours!'

He scattered the contents of the wallet on Gino's couch like a millionaire shedding banknotes: a well-worn passport, luggage labels, books of flimsy travel tickets—all the paraphernalia of adventure.

'I've thought of everything. Gino is on my passport now. It was his birth certificate I wanted from the Browns, not that blasted money. And I know yours is in order. You mentioned a trip to Paris with your school last year. We have reservations on the night flight to Milan, but from there I'm afraid it's a slow stretch by train to Ancona, unless we hire a car. We'll do whatever you think is best for Gino.'

They looked at her, the man and the little boy, their eyes shining with the same excitement and hope.

'Well, Sheila, what do you say?'

Sheila said: 'I think you must be out of your mind.'

'No, this is the soundest good sense. I've thought out every step. Listen.' And he told her the plan. Then again he and the boy waited, their eyes on her face.

Her throat tight, Sheila said: 'I still think it's crazy. You can't seriously believe I'd walk out of my hospital job—just like that—and fly to Italy?'

'Is it such an impossible thing to ask?' Victor said, and his eyes had gone dull and full of pain.

Because, of course, to one woman it hadn't seemed impossible. Giovanna had been willing to leave everything and follow him to the ends of the earth. The difference was, Giovanna loved him!

'Don't you see,' said Victor, pacing restlessly about again, 'it isn't a sacrifice. I'm asking you to exchange a depressing job in a building that looks and smells like a prison for a world of sunshine, flowers, music. . . . God, I wish I could show you that place!'

But words were clumsy things; barriers, not bridges; they were no use to him at such a moment. He snatched up his violin from its case and passed caressing fingers over the strings, then frowned, finding the A string sharpened by the heat of the room. He went over to the piano, gave himself the note and listened, head bent, till he was perfectly in tune. Then he reached for the bow and began to play.

Before Sheila's inward eye a sapphire sea sparkled, she saw the sardine nets hung out to dry on the red rocks, heard the wind sigh in the stone pines and drive forth fragrance from the lemon blossom. Gino laughed aloud, for now his father was playing one of the little folk tunes recorded in his musical box, giving it a lilting enchantment.

The door opened, Frank came in; he stood smiling a moment, then picked up his clarinet and felt his way into the thread of the melody. Lena, following him in with her coffee tray, dumped it on the floor. Then she was at the piano, her arm out of the sling. The three of them were at the work they loved most; improvising on the theme of the little folk tune, discovering exciting harmonies, thrilling changes of key, tossing the melody from one to another. Gino laughed aloud, stepping straight into this magic world of theirs.

It was crazy and wonderful. Sheila thought of the ward where everyone had been running round in panic, hunting for Gino. By now they'd have passed round her message and the day's work would get into its stride, regulated by meal times, the dressings trolley, the doctor's round, exactly like the turns of watch aboard ship.

This afternoon Stephen's form-master would be there: a lean, eager young man in a shabby jacket with leather patches on the elbows, but with incomparable riches stored in his head. 'It comes out at his eyes and ears like fireworks from a Guy Fawkes,' Nurse Connell reported, having brought the young man a cup of tea when he was wrestling with Stephen's mathematics. Miss Furlong would be there, too, gaunt and beaky, the tatty and beloved books of fairy stories tucked incongruously under her arm. It wasn't only Joe Porson who stood in need of her prayers today. . . .

They all passed in procession before her mind's eye, these busy people who helped her to fulfil Dr Gannet's dream that children in hospital should not be cut off from everyday, happy things; that life should flow through in a strong tide. And that left her with Timothy Redfern. She thought of him with a terrible longing. He had made Marbury General his world for the sake of a child who had died. Could she hope that he would understand and forgive what she did for Gino's sake today?

* * *

Summer dusk, a dark blue silken sky, the airport blazing with lights. Sheila saw none of this. Her head whirled with the hasty preparations for the journey, and when she saw how exhausted Gino was already she dreaded the outcome. Yet surely it was right, surely it was the only way! And she had the Chief's blessing on it. . . . She had tried to get in touch with Red, too, but he had left Scadcroft when she phoned. Perhaps it was as well. There was no knowing what he might have said or done!

After delays, the flight had been called at last. Now the luggage tender was backing away from the tail-end of the plane and the passengers were mounting the steps to the cabin. At that moment a service jeep raced across the airstrip. Rules were waived for a doctor on business, and Timothy Redfern had told them it was a matter of life and death. He was out of the jeep before it stopped, his eyes on the passengers entering the plane. A honeymoon couple, an elderly business man, a thin woman burdened with hand-luggage, then Victor Cort carrying his little boy wrapped in blankets. Sheila, slim in her flecked green linen suit, her bright brown hair blowing, was at the foot of the steps, talking earnestly to one of the officers. She was carrying a night-stop bag and a violin case. Victor reached the top of the steps and the air hostess reached out willing hands to take the child from him. Sheila called out something to them and started up the steps.

'Sheila! Stay where you are!' Red's voice halted her like a shot fired across the bows of the ship. Victor was just taking the violin case from her, handling it as tenderly as he had handled the child. She thrust the night-stop bag on to him, too, then turned round. Red's hand closed on her arm like a vice, his eyes were blazing with anger. The next moment he was hurrying her away from the plane. She struggled to free herself. The steps were moved away, there was the ear-cracking roar of the propellers and the mighty rush of wind. With tears running down her cheeks, Sheila was waving frantically to faces she saw only as a blur against the lighted windows of the cabin. They were airborne, and the night took them from her.

Red said tautly: 'I'm sorry it had to be this way. I'd have missed you altogether if the flight hadn't been delayed for a report on the weather conditions over the Alps.'

Sheila stared at him numbly, the tears bright on her cheeks. His hands tightened on her arms.

'I couldn't even give you the choice. I had to act. I knew, when it came to the point, your father's need of you would have first place.'

She blanched with sudden fear. 'My father!'

'Steady on. I exaggerated a bit when I told these people it was a matter of life and death. Your father has had another heart attack, a mild one. He's over the critical moment already, but of course he'll be kept under observation in the hospital for a week or two. He's asking for you. Your mother's there with him.' A pause. Then, in a queer, strained voice: 'The last thing they have in mind is to break up a romantic elopement! We've spared them that detail.'

She stiffened between his hands, stared at him for a long moment.

'Who told you?'

'Ilse. An hour ago. She had Mrs Tatlow in for treatment recently, and——' He finished savagely: 'Women and their gossip!'

Ilse, of course!

Dully angry, sick at heart, Sheila allowed herself to be helped into the jeep. Then there was the black and silver Jaguar waiting and a swift, empty road stretching ahead of them. Red drove in savage silence, his eyes fixed on the windscreen. When he spoke at last it was to say jerkily: 'Your father will soon be on an even keel again and you'll be catching another plane to Milan.'

He glanced round and saw her crying silently. It was too much for him. He drew into the next lay-by and took her in his arms.

'I can't bear it. I love you so terribly. You may as well know the truth. Even without the excuse of your father's illness I'd have dragged you off that plane.'

'Oh, thank goodness,' sobbed Sheila against his shoulder. She raised a tear-stained face. 'But you're making a dreadful mistake. I was only waving good-bye. It's Lena Tatlow who's travelling with them, to take care of Gino on the long journey to his mother's people.'

Red went very still. His eyes seemed to search her soul.

'Was that Cort's idea?'

She had to shake her head. 'No, it was mine. It came to me suddenly when those three were making music together. You see, on his way from Vienna, Victor had an impulse to see Giovanna's village again. Her parents long for their grandchild, and the little sister who was her maid of honour at the festival of the sea is grown-up and married now and will take Gino into her family and love him. Victor's idea was that I should take care of him on the trip, and he hoped . . . he thought——' She stopped rather suddenly and tried again. ' He actually thought I'd throw up my job—just like that and . . . and——' She floundered again, finishing desperately: ' But for Lena, who's always worked so hard and may never get the chance of such a wonderful holiday again, I knew it really would be the adventure of a lifetime. And so——' His kisses stopped her; for a moment of unbelievable happiness the world outside ceased to exist, dropping into a deep blue void like the night sky beyond the airport lights—Gino, and all her heart-searching over his future; her hospital job, her father's sudden illness, Ilse. . . .

Ilse. Why was she so confident of her hold on Timothy Redfern? Was there some promise between them, some bond?

Red felt the girl's lips tremble, her body shrink from his. Flattening herself into her corner, she said: ' Please, let's get back. And quickly. Quickly.'

He drove on without a word towards the sullen orange glow that hung over the city.

CHAPTER XIV

James Thorne was an awkward patient from the start.

According to the Ward Sister he was feeling better much too soon. He resented being in hospital at all and received their warnings about ever again going hell for leather at his gardening by saying that though he could grow prize vegetables he didn't fancy living like one. The only feature of hospital life he enjoyed was the company of other men, which he had missed since his retirement.

He told Sheila that her friend ' this big chap with the sea in his eyes ' looked in quite often to see him and spent some time with him every evening. ' But so far he has never once been lucky.'

'If you mean what I think you mean, Daddy, it's nonsense,' Sheila said with firmness. 'Doctor Redfern can see me any old time in the Children's Ward.'

'Ah, but that's in business hours! Not the same thing at all.' He gave his daughter a searching look and changed the subject. 'You could do something for the chap over there in Bed Eighteen. He works on the roads. Never learned to read and write. He's quite used to signing papers with his mark, but it shames him that Sister has to read his wife's letters and write the message in reply.'

So Sheila stretched the duties of ward teacher and wrote to the army education people for their primer. Recruits who couldn't read or write were one of their little problems. Soon she had Number Eighteen toiling away at his A B C, a huge fist clenched round a pencil, sweat standing out on his brow. Great was the rejoicing when he laboriously spelled out his first page of the primer, which began: 'How are you, Bill? Let us go and have a quick one, pal.' The army equivalent of 'The cat sat on the mat'!

He confided to Sheila that 'on the job' he always bought a newspaper and propped it up in front of him as he ate his dinner, like the other chaps. 'And now I'll be able to read all the bad news; what do you think of that, miss?'

Her father had found a real friend in his bed neighbour, Thomas Dodge, though it would be a long time before they had a quick one together. Mr Dodge was chief clerk to a firm of solicitors, Niblett & Barting, and Mr Niblett came to see him one afternoon when Sheila had looked in after school. There was an exchange of polite remarks in which she was amused to see the legal mind at play. For Mr Niblett was extremely careful not to sound too hopeful, in case this pair were really a lot worse than they looked, nor too depressing, in case they were lying there secretly dreading the worst.

With a certain relief he looked at his watch, having

timed himself exactly to a five-minute visit, and said: 'I have splendid news for our client Mrs Devon, Dodge. Splendid! A settlement at last. If she's anywhere around I'll get it signed and witnessed and that'll save me an evening call at her flat. I suppose she'll want Doctor Redfern to vet it first. Perhaps he's available, too.' He picked up his beautiful bowler hat and beamed at Mr Dodge. 'By calling to see you I can kill two birds with one stone.' That struck him as unfortunately worded and he coughed hastily. 'Let us say I shall be lucky if I can settle a little matter of business while engaged on an errand of mercy!'

'You will, sir, you will,' said Mr Dodge, and as his principal hurried away he chuckled. 'Serendipity. That's what he suffers from. It would fox all your clever doctors!'

'Serendipity?' repeated Sheila, mystified. She began to see why her father found Thomas Dodge such an entertaining companion.

'Lucky at picking things up,' translated Mr Dodge. 'Sixpences in the grass. And a real good meaty legal case when he thought he was merely going to collect ten and sixpence for communicating a client's dying wish to a friend.'

He lay back enjoying Sheila's reaction to this remark, then slowly winked.

'I don't know if a settlement is such splendid news to the lady in this case!' He lowered his voice, so that his words seemed to hiss and buzz like a busy telephone wire. 'Her husband met his end in a shocking street accident, as I expect you've heard. So young, too. A grand young fellow only just nicely established in medical practice in this city. Big quiet house, splendid situation for a young man putting up his brass plate. . . . In the old days, you know, and by that I mean the days before the National Health Service, the goodwill of a practice was something the widow could negotiate, but that's all changed. Oh, yes, it's all very complicated indeed.'

His voice, thought Sheila, seemed to be rubbing its hands. A matter, Mr Dodge seemed to suggest, so complicated that it was right up the street of Niblett & Barting.

'Also, the lorry-driver tried to make out that the doctor got out of his car in a negligent manner. All my eye. The lorry came so close, it tore off the car door. However, the claims have been to and fro for counsel's opinion. We have a big file on it. And of course it all takes time. Do you know, when I was rushed in here with my gastric trouble, I remember thinking as they lifted me on the stretcher: Now I shall never see the Devon case settled.'

'And all this time poor Ilse has been waiting——' Sheila put in, her voice high and jerky.

'Don't get the wrong idea, my dear young lady. Quite apart from this question of settling up the practice and receiving compensation for the fatal accident, Mrs Devon was left quite nicely off. Mark Devon inherited a tidy sum when his father died, and I may say it was placed in very nice investments. His widow hasn't been in want. Oh, dear, no. She needn't go on working. It's her own choice, and a sound one, of course. But the crux of the matter is this. Mark Devon died in the ambulance on his way to hospital, and he was conscious long enough to express the wish that his friend Timothy Redfern should "take care of Ilse". The words were passed on to us by Mrs Devon, who had them from the ambulance attendant, and I myself drafted the letter communicating his friend's dying wish to Doctor Redfern. We thought there might be difficulty in finding him as he had gone to sea a couple of years before. But in fact he was on the point of taking up a post here at M.G.H., so our task was simple.'

There was a pause. Sheila sat very still, her hands tightly joined in her lap.

James Thorne said: 'They'd been close friends, I gather?'

'Oh, yes, very close. And it's no secret that Timothy Redfern hoped to marry Ilse and was terribly cut up when she passed him by. Off the record, I believe Mark knew that and sent his dying message in the belief and hope that his friend still loved the girl and they'd make a go of it, after all. I daresay Ilse thought the same. But they were wrong, you know. It's been clear, all the time Doctor Redfern has been coming to our office on Ilse's behalf and standing by her in the negotiations for a fair settlement, that though he felt in duty bound to carry out the last wishes of his friend, his feelings towards the woman in the case had changed completely during his years away from Marbury.' He coughed. 'This is highly indiscreet!'

Sheila's eyes were fixed burningly on him, willing him to go on. He coughed again.

'You understand, this has been an awkward case. Profitable, but awkward. Just the sort of thing that brought on my gastric trouble. Often and often Mrs Devon has deferred some simple matter so that she could discuss it with Timothy Redfern, or she has made an appointment for Mr Niblett at an awkward time, taking up his whole evening. Of course his time is costly, but that didn't seem to worry her. I've had the feeling she was fighting for something beyond a financial settlement.' He pushed his lips in and out and made a deprecating gesture with his hands. 'A clever woman can put a young man of strict honour in a very tricky position indeed.'

'Dodgy,' James Thorne suggested; but his friend was sensitive about puns on his name and pretended not to hear.

'You know, Miss Thorne, some women do it with eyeshadow and a touch of perfume behind the ears. Ilse Devon tried red tape and sealing wax.'

'Hullo there!' Timothy Redfern loomed up at the foot of the bed. 'Just looked in as I was passing.'

Sheila could see her father thinking it was quite a

detour. Ward Seven and the Children's Unit were as the poles apart. He looked hard at his daughter, who had jumped up and seemed on the point of flight, her cheeks deeply flushed.

'Oh, dear me, dear me!' said Mr Dodge. 'My principal most particularly wants to see you, Doctor.'

'But I don't particularly want to see him,' said Red.

He held Sheila with an urgent, imploring look. The desire to run away suddenly left her. She met his glance.

'Then don't. The thing is settled at last. You're free of it.' She finished, very low, so that only Red heard. 'The debt of honour is paid.'

Across her father's bed she was smiling at him with all her heart in her eyes.

* * *

There were two events in the year for which the Children's Ward at Marbury General was 'dressed overall' and routine thrown overboard. One was Christmas and the other, by tradition, was Sister Bain's birthday. It had started years ago, Sheila was told, when the Registrar of that day brought along a bottle of sherry to celebrate passing his 'Membership' in Edinburgh and Sister Bain, mistaking his intention, had thanked him prettily for the birthday present. She protested every year that she preferred 'no fuss at all'. What woman wanted the whole hospital to keep tabs on her age? But in fact she enjoyed the occasion immensely and secret preparations, to which she turned an eye as blind as Nelson's, began weeks beforehand.

Sheila had the children painting greeting cards of their own design and practising songs and band items for the birthday concert. They had even grown a bouquet. Philip, the country child injured in the smash-up of his parents' car, certainly had green fingers, though his legs were no use to him whatever. He had riddled the soil for the window-boxes, pricked out the seedlings, watered and watched over them, and it was amazing what had come up: candytuft, marigolds, pansies with smooth purple faces, and little clumps of spotted persicaria. Sheila hadn't the heart to tell him his 'rare flower' was a weed growing there by mistake! The boxes were so full of colour, they were like the Italian brooches made of beads packed close together in patterns, and Philip had his eye on exactly the flowers he meant to pick for Sister's bouquet.

The chef had sent up a magnificent iced cake with so many candles that nobody could count them, which Sister said was just as well. And the Registrar had dipped into his own pocket and sent Nurse Connell shopping for toy balloons and party favours. He and Stephen put their heads together and ran up a signal in flags. The consultants always made a point of looking in to wish Sister a happy birthday, and this time Mrs Dee and Mrs Gannet came, too, because of the concert. Ilse sat with them, thus putting a gap between herself and the ward staff. If the children's voices were a little thin and wheezy and the percussion band rather hampered by splints and calipers, it was all the same a gloriously happy noise to Sheila's ears.

After the concert there was a special tea in Sister's office: frail sandwiches—not a vestige of crust for the birds—cream buns and shrimps and birthday cake, which somehow got handed round in the wrong order. Sheila had stayed on the ward, collecting up musical instruments and debris from the paper games, but Dick Sawley came looking for her.

'Here, stop lurking in the background! You're not cast for the role of Cinderella today. It seems they can't splice the mainbrace without you.'

'But we're still in the thick of the party. Jelly on all the sheets! I hope Sister knows Red bought the balloons and things?' They were his olive branch.

'Of course she knows. And she took care to spell out his signal before she let the visitors in. That woman

misses nothing! Off you go. I'll hold the fort here.'
He glanced round. 'Cor! How long does this caper go on?'

'Till the last balloon bursts.'

'That's easy. Give me a pin, somebody.'

'Och, and you're welcome, Doctor.' Nurse Connell had just come away from the babies and there were safety pins fastened to her dress like a row of medals.

'It's a shame, Dick. You ought to be having tea with the V.I.P.s,' said Sheila. Then she saw Eileen Connell giving him a lovely Irish smile and decided he wouldn't really miss the shrimps and cream buns.

She was just in time to see Sister open her birthday present, an elegant evening blouse with hand embroidery, which the Gannets had bought in Switzerland. 'Something for Sister,' Mrs Gannet said, was always at the top of her husband's holiday list.

'Oh, really, Doctor, you shouldn't,' said Sister Bain, glowing like a peony.

'My dear girl,' said Dr Gannet, for whom the years happily stood still, 'it's a small thing, when I think of the hard work you put in, running this chaotic place!'

'That's an odd sort of compliment,' said Mrs Gannet. She was wearing an amazing hat of pink chiffon with two huge roses bobbing at the front. The brim was rather large and it kept coming down over her eyes, giving her a rakish air. She put a hand on her husband's arm. 'Not quite so chaotic, surely, since you got your ward teacher?'

It was the cue for his little speech.

'I'm delighted with the teamwork on the ward. The occasion really speaks for itself. The greeting cards which the children designed themselves, the music, the flowers. It makes me very proud.' He glanced at Hamish Dee. 'Not to mention our young friend Stephen taking his examinations from a hospital bed!'

The *Marbury Gazette* had photographed Stephen when the exam results came through—Sister Bain and Sheila in the background, well disguised by the traction apparatus, and the model of a Bermudan-rigged sloop well to the fore.

'If children must be in hospital, then we have a clear duty to keep the link with home and school so that an illness or an operation isn't a permanent setback to the child's general progress. Redfern here will agree that the children are responding better to treatment now we're keeping them so busy, and the parents report less serious behaviour problems on the return home.'

He beamed round. And it was really such a tight squeeze in Sister's office, they were jammed close together, and Sheila could see Sister hoping the speech would be a brief one.

'I'd like you to remember the great Doctor Little—that London physician of the nineteenth century who persuaded his daughter to give simple lessons and handwork to the crippled children at his hospital, and so made her the first ward teacher. When we appointed Sheila Thorne I was confident she would carry on the same fine tradition—with the goodwill and support of my whole team. And I've been proved right. In fact, she——'

Ilse Devon's rippling laugh broke in. 'In fact, she's carrying the tradition far beyond M.G.H.!'

There was a startled instant when all eyes were on Ilse. To speak out of turn was a breach of etiquette, and actually to interrupt the Chief's speech was unheard of. Sheila felt dismayed, embarrassed, she dreaded what was still to come. For it seemed to her Ilse had lost control, some violent emotion drove her recklessly to focus attention on herself and spoil another woman's little moment of triumph.

'Did you know, Chief, she had me toting stuff over to Scadcroft? Paint and brushes and big sheets of cardboard. One can see there'd be more scope for her work there, of course, but the idea doesn't go over very well with Matron. I'm sorry about that.' Now she was turning to Sheila with a fixed little smile. 'Norina wasn't allowed to paint a frieze round her cubicle, so she did a huge poster and stuck it up. Flowers from every season all jumbled together. Rather pathetic, really. And bang in the middle, in big letters, she painted: I DIG RED.'

Timothy Redfern blushed fierily, and the others laughed.

Ilse added dryly: 'So Matron has switched her to gardening.'

Happily unaware of what was going on beneath the surface, Mrs Gannet exclaimed: 'How good of you both to take an interest in the child. If she has talent it should be encouraged. Couldn't she do some sketching out of doors? I really must hunt up the little easel I have tucked away in some corner. Every time we go abroad I mean to paint, and there's never time! But this young girl with time on her hands, and in need of sun and fresh air. . . . By the way, there was that handsome little boy who had to be flown to Italy for the sake of the climate. The one whose father is such a brilliant musician. How is he doing?'

She meant it so well, thought Sheila, agonized. She wanted her husband's team to know that she appreciated their work, and she let cats out of bags, dropped bricks, trod on toes. . . . With a terrific effort, Sheila smiled at her, and said in a low, hurried voice that Gino had stood the journey better than they hoped and was settling down happily with his Italian cousins.

Ilse butted in again. Why not ask her these things? Her information was more up-to-date than Sheila's. Lena Tatlow had been for treatment to the stiff arm since she returned from Italy and had given her the news that Victor had been signed up by one of the big Continental recording companies and his very first disc was a smash hit. All Rome was whistling, humming and twisting to some old folk song he had arranged, his swinging fiddle giving it a fascinating new rhythm.

'Ah! Dr Gannet nodded. 'Splendid news. But of course the main thing is that the child will be cared for and loved.'

Sheila's voice put in eagerly: 'And when he's the right age, perhaps some cardiac surgeon like Mr Bracewell——'

Her voice faltered off. Across the tea-things, Red met her eyes, his own holding strength and tenderness and complete understanding. Who else could know so well the anguish of mind she had lived through for a child's sake?

Ilse intercepted that look. It told her more plainly that if Niblett & Barting had couched it in legal terms and delivered it signed and sealed that the losing battle she'd been waging all these months was quite, quite over.

Dr Gannet chuckled quietly.

'I must say it seemed a crazy idea when you phoned me for a decision. I mean, with the child still so precarious. But when you assured me a nurse would be travelling with them, that settled it.'

Sheila's cheeks burned. 'What I actually said——'

'No matter. I confess I have only the haziest recollection of what happened that day. My cold—a most virulent germ—was at its worst and the new cure I was trying made me feel groggy. In fact, it was much worse than the original complaint!'

'Let that be a lesson to you,' said his wife. Smiling happily round, she confided: 'The drug houses send these samples, you know, and Alexander can't resist trying them out. He tries everything, I assure you. Gargles and inhalants, sleeping tablets and pep pills, appetite depressants that help you to lose weight and tonics that give you a keener appetite. And of course, indigestion powders galore.'

The Chief had gone turkey red. In her delightful, scatty way Mrs Gannet had betrayed his secret weakness. He hurried her out, and the party was over.

Yet not quite over. In the Children's Ward, as Sheila had discovered, nothing ever stood still.

Philip's parents had been discharged today from the cottage hospital and the vicar of their parish ran them to Marbury to see their boy. They arrived without warning at the most hectic moment, with the party debris being cleared away and the babies tuning up for their six o'clock feed. Sister had to give them tea and Philip, bedtime or no bedtime, must show off his flowers. It was tricky. Philip's parents had introduced the vicar as a keen gardener, a judge at country flower-shows, and Sheila actually held her breath when he put on his 'other' glasses to admire the window-box nearest to Philip's bed.

'Ah! Your iberis is doing well, I see. Candytuft is such a charming, old-fashioned name for it. And—um—polygonum persicaria. I have never seen it growing in a window-box garden before. It has the beauty of surprise.'

The beauty of surprise. Love was like that, Sheila thought. It had grown in her heart quite by chance, and now, in flowering, it made her see all beauty, all experience, with new eyes.

She and Red visited Ward Seven that evening. James Thorne had been in hospital much longer than expected. Red assured him the physician just wanted to make sure he was 'on an even keel'. Tonight they had good news for him. He was to go home tomorrow—in Red's black and silver Jaguar—leaving poor Mr Dodge disconsolate. They had more personal news for him that was not for Thomas Dodge's ears, so they plugged in his headphones and made him listen to a dull talk on 'Investments and the Law' while they got on with it, ignoring his acid remark about sons-in-law and serendipity.

Afterwards, as they crossed the hospital yard, Red slipped an arm round her and they paced slowly in the dusk, spinning out a brief and precious moment together before Red went back to do his evening round.

He said: 'I've been thinking how providential it was —and what courage it took—to phone the Chief at his home, against all rules and regulations, and needle him into giving his consent to Gino's air journey. Just imagine what Porson—I beg his pardon, Councillor Porson—would have made of the scandal if it got to his ears, from a quarter unnamed, that a child had actually been kidnapped from the ward and whisked across the Alps. Of course, he still has one titbit to chew over. Scandalous behaviour of Senior Registrar on hospital premises!'

'Well, it was scandalous,' said Sheila.

He gave her a merciless pinch. 'Don't you dare pretend I forced my attentions on you. Did you scream? Did you struggle when I kissed you? No. You closed your eyes and gave me your lips. It's true I was nearly out of my mind with love of you. But you were losing sleep over me, too.'

'Well!' It came out in an indignant squeak. 'If you want to know what I really thought of you at that time——'

'Go ahead. I can take it.'

She gave a soft little laugh and her hand came up shyly to touch his cheek.

'I thought you a slavedriving tyrant with salt in your veins.'

'Look, human blood is a saline solution in the proportion——'

She stopped him, her fingers over his mouth.

'There you go! Insufferably clever and superior! But in spite of everything, I do love you.'

His arms closed round her tightly. He drew her into a shadowy doorway.

'And in spite of everything, the Chief is going to have to find another ward teacher. Now that your parents are in the secret, suppose we ring up old Porson and give him the news? That'll take the wind out of his sails. He'll stutter and choke. Then he'll start preening himself because we thought him such an important chap we let him know before the chairman. He'll be forced to congratulate us and let his scandal drop.'

Sheila murmured: 'He'll think the grace of God has grabbed him when he wasn't looking.'

Red found the remark obscure. He went to the trouble of explaining his point of view.

'Even a Registrar surely has the right to kiss his bride-to-be on hospital premises.' His voice became an urgent whisper against her hair. 'Oh, dear heart, why not here and now?' He kissed her. It was a hunger and a passion and a glory.

Beyond the bounds of their new secret world the hospital lights shone out. In the Children's Ward the nurses were haring round, making ready to hand over to the night staff. Sister Bain was seated at her table writing up the book and making a note opposite new cases and those needing special vigilance.

Nurse Velta was walking up and down, rocking in her arms a tiny child who mustn't be allowed to cry because it might wreck a delicate surgical repair.

'Hush, baby, hush!' And then, when no one was listening: 'Ay, ay, sassy old devil pain done go fly away soon. Oh, lordy, yes! Tomorrow honey child done go laugh and sing. Tomorrow! Oh, lordy, yes! That sure will be the day!'

FREE! Harlequin Romance Catalogue

Here is a wonderful opportunity to read many of the Harlequin Romances you may have missed.

The HARLEQUIN ROMANCE CATALOGUE lists hundreds of titles which possibly are no longer available at your local bookseller. To receive your copy, just fill out the coupon below, mail it to us, and we'll rush your catalogue to you!

Following this page you'll find a sampling of a few of the Harlequin Romances listed in the catalogue. Should you wish to order any of these immediately, kindly check the titles desired and mail with coupon.

To: HARLEQUIN READER SERVICE, Dept. N 409
M.t O Box 707 Niagara Falls N.Y 14302
Canadian address: Stratford, Ont., Canada

☐ Please send me the free Harlequin Romance Catalogue.

☐ Please send me the titles checked.

I enclose $_____ (No C.O.D.'s). All books are 60c each To help defray postage and handling cost, please add 25c.

Name _____

Address _____

City/Town _____

State/Prov. _____ Zip _____

Have You Missed Any of These *Harlequin Romances?*

- [ ] 409 HOSPITAL CORRIDORS
  Mary Burchell
- [ ] 427 NURSE BROOKS Kate Norway
- [ ] 431 THE SILENT VALLEY
  Jean S. Macleod
- [ ] 438 MASTER OF SURGERY
  Alex Stuart
- [ ] 458 NEXT PATIENT, DOCTOR
  ANNE, Elizabeth Gilzean
- [ ] 487 THE HAPPY ENTERPRISE
  Eleanor Farnes
- [ ] 492 HOSPITAL PRO,
  Marjorie Moore
- [ ] 503 NURSE IN CHARGE
  Elizabeth Gilzean
- [ ] 516 PRISONER OF LOVE
  Jean S. Macleod
- [ ] 584 VILLAGE HOSPITAL
  Margaret Malcolm
- [ ] 683 DESIRE FOR THE STAR
  Averil Ives
  (Original Harlequin title "Doctor's Desire")
- [ ] 684 DOCTOR ON HORSEBACK
  Alex Stuart
- [ ] 699 THE HOUSE ON BRINDEN
  WATER Nan Asquith
  (Original Harlequin title "The Doctor Is Engaged")
- [ ] 701 DOCTOR'S LOVE Jane Arbor
- [ ] 711 MY HEART'S IN THE HIGH-
  LANDS Jean S. Macleod
- [ ] 723 FORTUNE GOES BEGGING
  Margaret Malcolm
  (Original Harlequin title "Nurse Langridge, Heiress")
- [ ] 779 MISTRESS OF BROWN
  FURROWS, Susan Barrie
- [ ] 796 HIBISCUS HOUSE,
  Fay Chandos
  (Original Harlequin title "Nurse Incognito")
- [ ] 850 THE OTHER ANNE,
  Caroline Trench
  (Original Harlequin title "Nurse Anne's Impersonation")
- [ ] 900 THERE CAME A SURGEON
  Hilda Pressley
- [ ] 1010 DOCTOR OF RESEARCH
  Elizabeth Houghton
- [ ] 1034 NURSE MEG'S DECISION
  Hilary Neal
- [ ] 1577 DR. MAITLAND'S SECRETARY
  Marjorie Norrell
- [ ] 1585 THE FLOWERING VALLEY
  Juliet Armstrong
- [ ] 1601 THE NEWCOMER
  Hilda Pressley
- [ ] 1639 THE VALLEY OF THE EAGLES
  Eleanor Farnes
- [ ] 1640 IF LOVE BE LOVE Flora Kidd
- [ ] 1644 WAYAWAY Dorothy Cork
- [ ] 1649 SWEET KATE Lucy Gillen
- [ ] 1652 A PEARL FOR LOVE
  Mary Cummins
- [ ] 1654 IN THE SHADE OF THE
  PALMS Roumelia Lane
- [ ] 1655 IT'S RUMOURED IN THE
  VILLAGE Mary Burchell
- [ ] 1657 WIFE TO SIM Joyce Dingwell
- [ ] 1702 A TOUCH OF MAGIC
  Essie Summers
- [ ] 1704 EXCEPT MY LOVE
  Mary Burchell
- [ ] 1705 THREE FOR A WEDDING
  Betty Neels
- [ ] 1729 THE YOUNG DOCTOR
  Sheila Douglas
- [ ] 1730 FLAME IN FIJI Gloria Bevan
- [ ] 1731 THE FORBIDDEN VALLEY
  Essie Summers
- [ ] 1732 BEYOND THE SUNSET
  Flora Kidd
- [ ] 1733 CALL AND I'LL COME
  Mary Burchell
- [ ] 1734 THE GIRL FROM ROME
  Nan Asquith
- [ ] 1735 TEMPTATIONS OF THE MOON
  Hilary Wilde
- [ ] 1736 THE ENCHANTED RING
  Lucy Gillen
- [ ] 1738 THE MUTUAL LOOK
  Joyce Dingwell
- [ ] 1739 BELOVED ENEMY
  Mary Wibberley
- [ ] 1740 ROMAN SUMMER, Jane Arbor
- [ ] 1741 MOORLAND MAGIC
  Elizabeth Ashton
- [ ] 1742 ALIEN CORN, Rachel Lindsay
- [ ] 1743 DESTINY IS A FLOWER
  Stella Frances Nel

All books are 60c. Please use the handy order coupon.

A